Table of Contents

Memorare

"Remember, O most gracious Virgin Mary, that never was it known that anyone who fled to thy protection, implored thy help, or sought thy intercession was left unaided. Inspired by this confidence, I fly to you, O Virgin of virgins, my Mother. To thee I come, before thee I stand, sinful and sorrowful. O Mother of the Word Incarnate! Despise not my petitions, but, in thy mercy, hear and answer me.

Amen."

"This book is dedicated to Our Lady of Martyrs Shrine, Auriesville, New York. The shrine is truly sacred ground."

Acknowledgement

I want to thank Sherrie Jo Bettles for all her work in editing, typing, and consulting on this book. God must truly love such a sweet, capable person – I know I do.

"Mary is the most sweet bait, chosen, prepared, and ordained by God, to catch the hearts of men"
-St. Catherine of Siena

Introduction

The central message of this book is the validity of Marian apparitions. There are incredible ramifications for Christians over this reality. Christians cannot take lightly the actual manifestation, and intercession, of the Mother of God (Jesus).

A cynical view towards this phenomenon is that the Catholic Church promotes apparitions to further its own aims. This is absolutely not true. The Roman churches actually very much down plays these matters. It pursues a very exacting, and lengthy investigation process in these Marian apparitions. Small percentages have actually been validated by the church. An appendix to this report includes the majority of these occurrences, and their status as to being accepted as genuine.

It should also be noted that over and above the validity of Marian apparitions, Christians in general need to realize the real spiritual nature of our world! Protestants especially need to acknowledge this reality. I have to admit it has always struck me as intellectually dishonest to play at being a Christian, and to think elements of the supernatural do not exist. Our primary emphasis is faith in Jesus and the biblical message. However, can Christians really think that angels, demons, visitations - all just disappeared?

Speaking as one whom many years ago had an exorcism, I can say with certainty the supernatural exists! The Christian religion is really not the intellectual exercise that liberal Protestant denominations like to portray it as. It is the war between cosmic good and evil.

We should not be so quick to dismiss the testimony of reliable witnesses. Not just in religious matters, but in almost all things, we have to believe what someone else tells us. The entire Gospel account itself is based on witness testimony. Even those agnostics, who believe in nothing but science, rely on their beloved scientists for truth.

Every message, related to the apparitions of the Virgin Mary, is one that points to belief in her son. Jesus spoke of Mary as our mother as well as His. (John 19:26-27) Protestants need to have a little courage. This is true even if it challenges their perspectives. A fair reading of the gospel of John would give Mary a high status, regardless whether the reader is Catholic or Protestant.

It is important that one grasp the seriousness and thoroughness the Roman Catholic Church uses to evaluate apparitions. There have only been 10 apparitions that have been given full Church approval. They are:

1. Guadalupe
2. Laus
3. Rue De Bac
4. Banneaux
5. Beaurang

6. Knock
7. Lourdes
8. Fatima
9 Zeitoun (Coptic)
10. Akita

These fall into a category that is considered to be of a "supernatural nature". Even in this higher category of church approval, it should be noted that a belief in apparitions is not mandatory for Christians. A visitation by Mary is a contact from God, but we can contact Him every day in prayer and church!

Still, God is using Mary as a messenger. It would be very dull of us to not be interested in God's demonstration of love, and attempt at contact!

The second category of approval of apparitions is where the event is evaluated by the local bishop. If the investigation by the bishop is positive, the apparition is considered to be "worthy of devotional expression". There have been dozens of apparitions that have fallen into this category.

The sacred congregation of the Doctrine of the Faith, in 1978, issued "Norms of the Congregation for proceeding in judging alleged apparitions and revelations." These approaches were given full Vatican approval.

There are really three categories that are evaluated in terms of approval of an apparitional event:

1. First, there has to be a high probability that a supernatural (miraculous) event has occurred. An investigation of the seers, witnesses and location are all involved.
2. Second, the church has to evaluate the mental soundness of the seers, as well as their honesty. For example; are the seer's loyal parishioners, drug takers, or economic opportunists?
3. Finally, the church evaluates the messages received to determine theological soundness. The messages must uphold basic Catholic doctrine. One would hardly think that the messages were from God if the suggestion was given, say, to go out and get divorced!

Spiritual benefit would have to be positive within the apparition. The messages from Mary are almost invariably to underscore God's love, and to give hope. Even when the message has apocalyptic warnings, there is usually an offer of mercy if we repent!

Pope Benedict XIV said of the apparitions: "Even though many of these revelations have been approved, we cannot and ought not give them the assent of divine faith, but only that of human faith, according to the dictates enable us to decide that they are probable and worth of pious credence".

The church is being cautious because it does not want our faith to be undermined by a fraudulent event. However, various Popes have visited apparitional sites. Pope John Paul II visited Knock and Lourdes, for example. This of course is a tacit approval of the events' validity.

It seems from various sources and insights that we are due a paradigm shift. When I was growing up in the 1960's, there was a strong current of the "God is Dead" movement. I remember, as a student minister, overhearing veteran ministers discussing the overview of their beliefs. The tone of their conversations was a somewhat smug attitude. One got the idea that they were embarrassed at even discussing a reality that involved supernatural events.

This attitude was resultant, I think, from several sources. First, there was the "God is dead" movement. This was really just mankind's arrogance over having a little technological success. I remember one of the texts from the United Methodist Church spoke of Jesus and His resurrection. The text basically said that if one believed that Jesus was the real thing, Son of God etc., or just a fine philosopher; it was all to the good. Of course, even a non-religious person would obviously be aghast at such an attitude. In other words, why should we pose as a minister if you don't even believe in the basics? It was all I could do not to call these hypocrites what they were.

I mention these things because I am trying to demonstrate a mind-set. It does not have to be as extreme as the previously mentioned ministers. Jesus said we should be in this world, but not of it. Too often, we are "of it".

We really don't know much of anything except things are a lot more complex than we initially thought they were. There is even a debate over whether oil results from decomposed dinosaurs (fossil fuel), or a geological process. (Jerome Corsi, PhD in "Black Gold Stranglehold").

The top theoretical physicist of today is Michio Kaku. This City College of New York professor is a proponent of "string theory". This speaks of a multi-verse, as opposed to a universe. This includes a whole sea of realities that were not taught in the classical physics class. Examples would include parallel universes, "worm holes", and dark matter. The latest finding, circa 2007, is the existence of dark energy. There are either eleven or twenty-six identified dimensions, depending on which theoretical physicist one listens to. There are surely more than our three dimensions!

It should also be remembered that Jesus went to minister to the angels at Tartarus after His death on the cross. Tartarus was a different Greek word than the "sheol" depiction of hell. The essence of this was that Jesus went to another dimension to deal with recalcitrant demons. In the same vein, does not Ephesians describe the Devil as "prince of the air"? These are more than just idle words as a description. It is not clear what the "air" is, but the implication is that it is not confined to our understanding of a place. Similarly, Jesus spoke of us having resurrection bodies where we could go and come at will. This facet clearly demonstrated physical properties that we can only be amazed at.

I have a friend in Major Paul Smith, U.S. Army, retired. This Austin, Texas resident was the primary trainer for the Army's Stargate Program. He is a frequent guest on national talk shows. His book, "Reading the Enemy's Mind", was serialized in Reader's Digest early in 2007. The Stargate Program was an ongoing effort to spy on America's enemies. It had a twenty-year life span through four presidents. It received commendations from the Customs Department for aiding in the location of drugs and drug smugglers.

In my conversations with Paul, he indicated that through all the exotic experiences with remote viewing, no conflicts arose among Christians and their beliefs. This does not mean very unusual experiences didn't occur over these efforts. Paul, a devout Mormon, had all manner of Christians for training. The thrust of his input was that even with all highest-level of emphasis on the effort, we really don't know why we have psychic capabilities.

Of all the knowledge mankind has, the best of it is the assurance of a loving God. I, and millions of others, have experienced answered prayer. I, and millions of others, have experienced supernatural "highlights" or proofs.

The Catholic Church itself says that it is not necessary to accept the validity of Marion apparitions. (Univ. of Dayton-Marion Research Institute). This applies even to events the church has validated. Jesus Christ's reality is the prime Christian emphasis.

The transfiguration was a form of apparition. Angels appeared to Lot, Mary, and others. God himself appeared to

Moses! Why does the notion of Mary appearing to present day Christians seem unlikely? I submit that her appearances are likely true events.

The Bible sets the basis for legal proceedings as two witnesses. One would have to look at the apparitional events at Zeitoun, Egypt, where literally millions were witnesses, plus visual televised evidence, far exceed any level of evidence necessary for a typical legal proceeding.

Another aspect of our skepticism, relative to these events, is over personal   testimony. We know very little of any area without personal testimony. The whole Bible itself hinges on the credibility of personal testimony. To reject out of hand human testimony is to degrade our view of humanity. It is a true saying that "all men are liars". However, all men are not liars at all times. I have never seen the continent of Europe, but it is undoubtedly there. The great preponderance of evidence supports Mary's reality.

Jesus speaks of Mary as our mother, as well as His. No one would expect us to be superstitious, seeing Mary in a "burnt piece of toast". But, when millions of credible witnesses see the Virgin Mary, made up of mixed Christian and Muslim components, it might be fitting to take our Mother seriously.

Chapter 1
Early Apparitions

Some of the apparitions in this book also include visits from angels and even Jesus Himself. The great Saint Catherine Labouré was blessed to have all three kinds of manifestations. Usually, the apparition is visual, though it can just be an internalized voice message. Often, the Virgin Mary characterizes her visits with a title, like "Our Lady of the Rosary", or "Mediatrix of All Graces".

The Virgin Mary has been appearing to Christians since the time before her death. This is no new fad or phenomenon. Importantly, it is not only a series of paranormal and divine events. Her role is part of a great love story. The love emanates from God Himself, through His Son Jesus, and down through Mary.

Jesus spoke of Mary as our mother, as well as His. (See John 19:26-27) Luke also contains the first "Hail Mary" in saying, "Hail Mary full of grace, blessed are you among women..." A fair reading, no matter what denominational stamp one bears, is that a maternal role has been assigned to her, relative to all of Christianity. By her visits, she conveys instructions, warnings and hope.

In 40 AD, James the apostle was having a difficult time evangelizing the local Spaniards. A legend has been passed down that the Blessed Virgin appeared to James at Saragossa, Spain. She appeared with a wooden statue of herself, as well as a pillar of Jasper wood. Thus, the apparition has been called "Our Lady of the Pillar".

Mary asked for a chapel to be built for her on this spot to commemorate her visit. Today there is a cathedral there called Compostella. Joan Cruz's book "Relics" has a photo of what is reported to be the original jasper wood pillar.

Our Lady of the Pillar was the earliest of recorded Marian apparitions. Also, it occurred while Mary was still alive! Even in this instance, Mary was acting like a mother consoling her Son's discouraged apostle.

The apostle John writes in Revelation 12:
" A great sign appeared in heaven: A woman clothed with the sun, with the moon under her feet, and a crown of 12 stars on her head. She was pregnant…but she gave birth to a Son-a male who is going to shepherd all nations with an iron scepter".

This imagery deals with no other female but the Virgin Mary. The apostle John had an apparition of Mary, but one of the internal kind of revelation. Note that the image he portrays of Mary is very close to the description many seers have reported. All this underscores that Mary was not just another woman, as an Anglican priest recently told me.

In the year 352 AD, Pope Liberius and a wealthy Roman couple, all had a dream where Mary asked them to build a church in her honor, on the Esquiline hill in Rome.

Upon visiting the hill, they saw where the snow formed the outline of a church. This is the current site of the Basilica of Saint Mary Major. In this visit, Mary has been referred to as "Our Lady of the Snows."

In 1061, the village of Walsingham in Norfolk, England was the site of an early Marian apparition. The Virgin Mary is reported to have appeared to Richeldis de Faverches, a wealthy Saxon noblewoman. In this vision, Mary asked the noblewoman to have a Holy House built. This was a replica of the house where the Holy family resided. Mary asked that a shrine by built in England to commemorate the annunciation.

This town in England became one of the greatest destinations for pilgrimages in Christendom. Many English kings visited this shrine, including all the Henry's from King Henry III to, ironically, King Henry VIII.

It was odd that Henry VIII was a pilgrim because it was at his order that the shrine was destroyed in 1538. This destruction came about as result of the English church reformation. (Caused by Henry's divorces)

Finally in 1897, Pope Leo XIII began the reconstruction of what is known as the Slipper Chapel. This is the Roman Catholic part of the shrine. The Church of England also rebuilt its version of the Holy House, adjoining the Slipper Chapel.

The last of the older apparitions is that of Our Lady of Mt. Carmel. This is not to say there were not others, but information is sketchy on many older apparitions. Actually, from what can be estimated; there have probably been several thousand apparitions. Many, as indicated, were for personal revelation.

In 1251, the Virgin Mary made her visit to Simon Stock. Stock, age 82, had been elected superior general of the Carmelite order that same year.

Mary appeared to Stock bearing an infant (Jesus) in one hand and a brown scapular in the other. (Note: A scapular is a rectangular piece of cloth with Mary's image on it) Her message was, "Take, beloved son, this scapular of thy order as a badge of my confraternity and for thee and all Carmelites a special sign of grace; whoever dies in this garment will not suffer everlasting fire. It is the sign of salvation, a safeguard in dangers, a pledge of peace and of the covenant".

The brown scapular has been perhaps the most widespread symbol of veneration of the Virgin Mary. It is memorialized in the annual feast of Our Lady of Mt. Camel on July 16.

These early apparitions do not have the physical proofs of later apparitions: documented cures, photos, thousands of witnesses, and physical evidence. They do, however, show that the Virgin Mary has had a role from the beginning, and scripture underscores this role.

Chapter 2
Our Lady of Guadalupe

This great apparitional event is considered the first of the modern age. As in other cases this occurred at a pivotal time in human history. Spain was the pre-eminent power in Europe, and was swiftly colonizing the new world. Cuba was first colonized under Christopher Columbus; then a western expansion proceeded in pursuit of gold.

Hernan Cortez arrived in Mexico in 1519. This extremely brave military leader lead 300 soldiers in an invasion of Aztec controlled territory. His force was outnumbered by thousands to one, yet he finally succeeded in taking the Aztec capital in 1521.

The Spanish were successful in part because the Aztec mythology included the expected arrival of white gods. This tempered what could have been a very disastrous response from the Indians.

Cortez' men actually behaved very little like gods. Rape and torture were pretty much the rule of the day. The Spanish felt the Indians were sub-human, and as such could be treated like slaves! The Indians were also looked upon in this matter because of an incredible practice of human sacrifice by the Aztecs.

The church tried to act as a check on the soldiers' brutality, but the effort was not very fruitful. The gold lust and Spanish arrogance were just about unstoppable forces. Fortunately, these virtually "unstoppable forces" were confronted with a truly unstoppable one-the great apparition of Mary to the Indian Juan Diego, in December, 1531.

Juan Diego, a local Indian convert to Christianity, was walking on Tepeyac Hill. This was near the current site of Mexico City. Juan heard "sweet singing", and went in the direction where it seemed to be coming from.

At the top of the hill, Juan saw a beautiful lady who beckoned him to come forward. She said, "Listen, Juan, dear, smallest of my sons, where are you going?". He answered that he was going to worship in the town of Tlatelolco.

Mary then said to Juan: "Know and understand, smallest of my sons! I am the ever-virgin, Holy Mary, Mother of the true God; the life-giving Creator of all people; the Lord of what is near and what is far, of heaven and earth. I deeply desire that a chapel be built to me here where I can show, praise and testify to Him forever. Here I will give people all my love, compassion, help, comfort and salvation. For I am truly your compassionate mother: your mother and the mother to all who dwell in this land, and to all nations and peoples who love me and call and entreat me. Here I will console them…"

The Blessed Virgin Mary asked Juan Diego to go to the bishop's palace, and to relay her desire for a chapel to be built on Tepeyac Hill.

Upon reaching town, Juan went to the residence of the bishop, Juan de Zumarraga. After pleading with the servants, he was finally allowed a brief audience with the bishop. He was essentially told to come back another time, no being taken seriously.

Juan went back to the hill, and begged Mary to send someone of greater stature to deliver the request. Mary said that she had many she could send, but it had to be Juan to deliver the message.

The next audience with the bishop was not much more productive. After intense "grilling" by the bishop, Juan was again sent away.

Juan again went to Mary, indicating the bishop's skepticism. Hearing this, the virgin told Juan to come back the next day to show the bishop a sign. The following day Juan Diego did not return to the hill because his uncle seemed to be at the brink of death. He decided, that next morning, to fetch a priest for his uncle.

In the process of fetching the priest, Juan again encountered the Virgin Mary. He told her he did not mean to disobey her, but was preoccupied with his dying uncle. Mary told him not to worry, that his uncle would be cured.

She told him to climb to the top of the hill where he first saw her, and gather the flowers growing there. (This was in December, when no flowers should be growing) He went to obey her instructions, and gathered the roses. Then, Juan brought them back to Mary. She told him the roses were the sign needed for the bishop. Juan, once again, got his audience with the bishop. They saw the roses, and a miraculous imprint of the Virgin Mary on his tulma (cloak). They were convinced of the legitimacy of the vision. The chapel is now the Basilica of Our Lady of Guadalupe, and still houses Juan's cloak- not deteriorated after almost 500 years!

The garment has been studied by the most famous physical testing labs in the world. Note-there is no evidence of tracing or pigment on the fragile cactus husk garment! Sandia Labs has confirmed the miraculous nature of the imprint, i.e. no pigment.

Another aspect of the analysis of the cloak is the image found in the Virgins eyes. This is a reproduction of the reflected image found in human eyes. In 1956, Dr. Javier Torroalla Bueno, ophthalmologist, verified the presence of the Samson-Purkinje effect. This the reflected image round in all human eyes. It is exactly similar to where the reflections would be in human eyes, and has similar distortion. The image is also found in both eyes.

Another analysis was undertaken in 1979 by Dr Jose Tonsman, a Cornell university PhD. These efforts included digital images that not only confirmed the earlier images, but found two more human figures. These images replicated the scene where Juan Diego showed the tulma to the Bishop and translator.

Since these analyses were made, over twenty ophthalmologists have verified the images in the Virgin's eyes. Modern skepticism notwithstanding, it seems the detail in this image negates any likelihood of fraud in the creation of the garments' image. The detail is way too fine for a human artist to duplicate, and there is no tracing or pigment! Skeptics do your best!

Antonio Valeriano's translation from Nahuatl (Aztec) in 1649 is as follows:

The complete 1649 text by Luis Lasso de la Vega of a narrative written by Antonio Valeriano a century before about the fantastic events surrounding the encounter of the Virgin Mary with a widower in December 1531.

Here is set forth in an orderly way the marvelous manner in which the ever-virgin Holy Mary, Mother of God, our Queen, lately appeared on Tepeyac Hill, now called Guadalupe. First she revealer herself to a poor Indian named Juan Diego; and later her precious image appeared before the new bishop Friar Juan de Zumarraga. And all the miracles she performed [will also be related].

Ten years after the conquest of the City of Mexico, shield and arrows were put aside, war ceased, and there was peace at sea and on land among the peoples, as faith began to spring up, knowledge of the true God through whom everything lives. At that time in the year 1531, a few days into December, there was a poor Indian known as Juan Diego, a native of Cuautitlan. Tlatelolco was the center of all things spiritual, and it was to there on this Saturday, long before daybreak, that he was walking to divine worship and praise.

As he reached the little Tepeyac Hill, dawn broke, and he heard singing up on the hill like the song of a variety of wonderful birds; sometimes the singers' voices were still, and then it seemed as if the mountain itself answered them. Their song was sweet and delightful, surpassing that of the *coyoltototl* and *tzinizcan* and other beautiful song birds.

Juan Diego stopped to attend to this and said to himself: "Am I worthy or deserving of what I am hearing? Or am I dreaming? Perhaps I will soon awake from this sweet dream. Where am I? Perhaps in the earthly paradise of which our ancestors have spoken? In this the country of flowers, the country of corn and fleshpots? Am I perhaps already in heaven?" He was looking eastward up on the hill from where the wonderful heavenly song was coming, when it suddenly ceased and all grew still. Then he heard someone calling him from up the hill: "Juan, dear. Dearest Juan Diego." He then ventured to go where the voice was calling him. At the top he saw a Lady standing there, telling him to come closer. Once in her presence he was astonished at her splendor, which surpassed anything he had ever seen. She was perfect; her dress was radiant as the sun; the stones and rocks on which she stood were shot through with brilliance, like a bracelet of precious stones, and lit the earth like a rainbow. The mesquite, prickly pear and other chaparral that grows there seemed like emerald; their foliage, fine turquoise; and their branches and thorns gleamed like gold.

He bowed to her and listened to her soft and courteous voice. Love and peace came from her. Her affection was compelling in drawing him to her. She said to him: "Listen, Juan, dear, smallest of my sons, where are you going?" He replied: "My Lady, my Queen, and my little girl, I am going to your house in Mexico-Tlatelolco, to praise and serve God as taught by our priests, the representatives of our Lord."

She then spoke to him and revealed her holy will: "Know and understand, smallest of my sons! I am the ever-virgin, holy Mary, Mother of the true God; the life-giving Creator of all people; the Lord of what is near and what is far, of heaven and earth. I can deeply desire that a chapel be built to me here where I can show, praise and testify to him forever. Here I will give people all my love, compassion, help, comfort and salvation. For I am truly your compassionate Mother: your Mother and the Mother to all who dwell in this land and to all over nations and peoples who love me and call and entreat me. I am the Mother of all who seek me and place their trust in me. Here I will hear their cries and listen to their complaints. Here I will console them in their suffering and relieve their pain. Here I will heal them in their anguish, their affliction and distress. To bring about all that my tenderness wants to achieve, go to the palace of the bishop of Mexico and tell him how I am sending you to make known to him my great desire that he build me a chapel there. On this flat place he should build me a chapel. Tell him in detail what you have seen, wondered at and heard. Know assuredly that I will reward you richly and will repay you. I will know how to thank you. Yes, I will make you happy and give you great joy. For the reward you will earn for this service is great. I will repay you for your labor and fatigue. Now, you have heard my command, my son, my smallest. Go and give your best effort to this task."

At this point, he bowed before her and said: "My Lady, my child, I am going to carry out the splendid command voiced by your perfect breath. I will say good-bye for now, I, your humble servant." Then he went down to carry out her orders, coming out of the path that was the direct route to Mexico. Upon entering the city, he went directly to the palace of the bishop; a prelate just recently arrived, named Friar Juan de Zumarraga, a religious of Saint Francis.

Arriving, he tried to see the bishop; he begged his servants to announce him. A long time later, they came to call him, as the bishop had ordered him brought in. As soon as he entered, he bowed and knelt before him; then he gave him the message of the heavenly Lady. He also told him all he had wondered at, seen and heard. After hearing his speech and the message, the bishop seemed not to take him seriously and responded: "Come back some other time, my son, and I will listen to you at greater leisure. I will consider from the very beginning all the reasons you have brought me and think about your wishes and desires."

He went away from there. Sad because he had not been able to carry out his task, he returned that very day to the top of the hill and was fortunate to find the heavenly Lady, who was waiting for him at the very spot where he had first seen her. Catching sight of her, he prostrated himself before her and said: "My Senora, Lady, Queen, smallest of my daughters, my littlest one, I went where you sent me immediately to carry out your orders voiced by your sweet breath. Although it was difficult, I gained entry to where the prelate was sitting; I saw him and gave him your message, as you instructed. He received me kindly and listened attentively, but by the way he responded it seemed that I had not been able to convince him. He said to me: 'Come back some other time, my son, and I will listen to you at greater leisure. I will consider from the very beginning all the reasons you have brought me and think about your wishes and desires.' By the way he responded, I understood perfectly well that he thinks that it is perhaps some invention of mine that you want them to build you a chapel and that the command did not come from your lips. Therefore, I earnestly beg you, my Lady and littlest child, to send one of the noblemen, someone who is known, respected and esteemed, to take your message, so that your mission will be accomplished and the words that come from your sweet lips will be believed. Because I am only a man of the fields, a poor creature. A piece of string, the tail-end, a peon, a slave, a rope, dirt, a leaf, the bottom of the pile. I must be led myself. I must be carried on the back. My littlest Virgin, smallest of my children, you have sent me to a place where I do not belong. My child! My Lady and Queen! I beg you to release me from your demand. For I am grieving your face and your heart. I will only cause disappointment and anger if I go, my Lady and mistress."

The venerable, most holy Virgin answered him: "Listen, my littlest one, my son! Understand that I have many servants and messengers whom I could send to deliver my message and do my will. But it is absolutely necessary that you yourself go and make the request. Through you mediation should my heart's wish and will be accomplished. I earnestly beg you, my son, my smallest, and strictly command you from my heart to go again tomorrow to see the bishop. Speak in my name, and make him understand completely my will that he begin construction of the chapel I am requesting. And tell him again that I, the ever-virgin, holy Mary, Mother of God, am sending you."

Juan Diego answered. "My Lady, Queen, my little one, let me not cause you pain or sadden your heart. Very willingly will I go to carry out this task, deliver the words of your breath. In no way will I neglect doing it or think the way too arduous; I will go to do your will, even though he may perhaps not want to hear me, or hears me but still does not believe. Tomorrow afternoon, when the sun goes down, I will come back to tell you the bishop's answer. And now I say good-bye to you, my little one, good Lady and Queen. My child! In the meantime, rest a little." Then he made his way home so that he, too, might rest.

The next day, Sunday, long before dawn, he left his house and went straight to Tlatelolco, to be instructed in the things of God, put his name on the list of the baptized, and see the bishop afterward. He arrived just before ten. He was ready. He went to Mass and had himself inscribed in the list of the baptized. The crowd had already dispersed when Juan Diego went to the bishop's palace. As soon as he arrived he made every effort to see the bishop and with great difficulty succeeded. He knelt at his feet and sadly wept as he repeated the command of the heavenly Lady – that he would believe the message and will of the Immaculate One that he should build a small chapel at the location that she had chosen. To get at the facts, the bishop asked him many things: where he had seen her and what she looked like. And Juan Diego gave a perfect accounting to the bishop. Even more, he described her precisely and all he had seen and wondered at, and how everything about her showed her to be the ever-virgin, most holy

Mother of the Savior, our Lord Jesus Christ. Still, the bishop did not believe him.

He told him that he could not do what he was requesting simply on his word and because of his insistence. It was very necessary to have a sign, so that he could believe that the heavenly Lady herself was sending him. As he listened, Juan Diego said to the bishop: "My lord, what sign do you want? I will go to the heavenly Lady who sent me and ask her for it." The bishop noted that he was consistent in his story, without uncertainties or hesitations, and then sent him away.

But right away he ordered some trustworthy people of his household to follow him and find out where he went and whom he saw and to whom he talked. They complied. Juan Diego come straight back along the path. Those who followed him lost him at the ravine near the Tepeyac Bridge; and although they looked for him everywhere, they never saw him. So they returned, not only because they were tired of searching, but also because they were frustrated, which made them angry. They went to report all those to the bishop' telling him not to put this faith in Juan Diego, as he was simply deceiving him; he was making up the story he had come to tell or perhaps had only been dreaming and what he had asked for was a fantasy. Finally they agreed that if he came again, he should be taken and punished severely, so that he would never again lie or deceive in order to create a sensation.

Meanwhile Juan Diego was with the most holy Virgin, giving her the bishop's answer. Upon hearing it, the Lady and Queen said: "Very well, my son, my dearest child, come back here tomorrow so that you can take to the bishop the sign of truth he has asked for. Then he will believe you and will stop doubting and being suspicious of you. And you, my little son, know that I will repay your concern and the work and fatigue tat you have expended for me. So go now. I will await you here tomorrow."

The next day, Monday, the day on which Juan Diego was supposed to take some sign back as proof, he did not return. For when he arrived home, he found that his uncle, Juan Bernardino, had fallen sick and already lay near death. First Juan Diego called a physician, but, in spite of the doctor's efforts, nothing more could be done, since he was so deathly ill. During the night his uncle begged him to go out, before daybreak, to Tlatelolco to call a priest who would hear his confession and prepare him for dying, because he was very certain that death was upon him and that he would never again rise or be healed.

Tuesday, long before daybreak, Juan Diego left his house for Tlatelolco, to call the priest. When he approached the path that follows the contours of Tepeyac Hill, along his usual route on the west side, he said to himself: "If I go straight, the Lady might see me and detain me, so that I take the bishop the sign of which she spoke. First, we have to deal with our affliction and call the priest. My poor uncle is anxiously waiting for him." He turned toward the hill and climbed it on the eastern side, so that he could get to Mexico more quickly without the heavenly Lady delaying him. He thought that from where he turned off, she, who sees well everywhere, would not be able to see him. At this very moment, he saw her coming down from the top of the hill, looking toward the spot where he had seen her before. She came to meet him at the side of the hill and said to him: "What is happening, my son, my smallest? Where are you steps headed? Where are you going?"

Was he a little embarrassed or ashamed to be startled? Or even scared or taken by fright? Juan Diego bowed before her and greeted her: "My little one, my dear little daughter, my child and my Queen! I hope you are happy. How are you today? Did you rest well, and has the day begun well? Are you in good health, my Lady and child? I have to cause you some pain, and that makes me sad. Know, my little girl that one of your poor servants, my uncle is very ill; he has a terrible sickness and is on the point of death. Now I am rushing to your house in Mexico to call one of the priests, beloved by our Lord, to go hear his confession and prepare him, for from the day of our birth, we approach the hour of a good death. When I have fulfilled my duty, I will be right back again to go again to take your message, my Lady and beloved child. Please forgive me. Have patience with me now. I am not deceiving you, my child, my smallest daughter. Tomorrow I will hurry back here to you."

After listening to Juan Diego's speech, the most kindly virgin answered: "Hear and understand my smallest and dearest son that what is alarming and afflicting you is nothing. Do not let your countenance or your heart be disturbed. Do not fear this illness or any other illness or suffering. Am I, your Mother, not here? Are you not under my shadow and protection? Am I not the source of your joy? Are you not in the folds of my mantle, in the crossing of my arms? What more do you need? Let nothing else disturb or distress you. Do not worry about your uncle's illness. He will not die from it today – be assured that he has been cured." (At that precise moment, his uncle was healed, as it was later learned.) When Juan Diego heard these words of the heavenly Lady, he was greatly reassured and was at peace. He begged her to send him as soon as possible to see the bishop and take him the sign and proof, so that he would believe.

The heavenly Lady then told him to climb to the top of the hill where he had seen her before, saying: "Climb, my son, my smallest to the top of the hill, where you saw me and received my errand. There you will find various flowers. Cut them, gather them and put them together. Then come right down and bring them before me." Juan Diego immediately climbed the hill and when he got to the top he was greatly astonished that so many varieties of exquisite Castilian roses had bloomed, with their petals wide open, so long before their season, for at this time of the year everything was covered with frost. They were very fragrant, drenched in dew that looked like precious pearls.

Right away he began to cut them and gather them up into the folds of his tilma. The top of the hill was certainly not the place where flowers bloomed. There were just stones, thistles and thorns, mesquite and cactus. Now and then herbs grew, but not in December, when the frost destroyed all life. He went down immediately, bringing the colorful flowers he had gone to cut to the heavenly Lady. When she saw them, she rearranged them with her precious hands and put them back in his tilma, saying: 'My son, my smallest, this variety of flowers is the proof and the sign you are to take to the bishop. Tell him in my name to see my desire in them and do my will and wish. You are my ambassador most worthy of my trust. I strictly command you to open your tilma and reveal what you carry only in front of the bishop. Give him a fill account. Tell him that I commanded you to climb to the top of the hill to cut the flowers; tell him all you have seen and wondered at, so that you can persuade the prelate to do what he can to make and erect the chapel that I have asked for."

After the heavenly Lady had advised him, he set out on the path that leads directly to Mexico. He was at peace and sure of a good outcome, holding with great care what he carried in his tilma, taking care to drop nothing and rejoicing in the fragrance of the variety of beautiful flowers. When he arrived at the bishop's palace, the porter and the other servants went out to meet him. He entreated them to tell the bishop that he wanted to see him, but not one of them would do so, pretending that they could not hear him – either because it was very early or because they perceived him as a nuisance or because their companions had told them about losing sight of him whey they had tried to follow him the day before.

He waited a long time. When they saw that he had been standing there a long time, barefooted, head bowed, not doing anything in case he were called, and noticed that he seemed to be carrying something in his tilma, they approached to see what he carried and satisfy their curiosity. So, in the end, Juan Diego let them glimpse the flowers because it was clear to him that he could no longer conceal his miraculous gift and in order to keep them from harassing him further or evicting or flogging him.

And when they saw that they were genuine Castilian roses, which did not bloom at that time of year, they were greatly astonished, since, besides, they were fresh-picked, completely open, very fragrant and very beautiful. They tried to grab and take some three times but had no luck, because, as they grabbed, the flowers no longer seemed real, but painted, embroidered, or appliquéd on the tilma.

They hurried to the bishop to tell him what they had seen and that the humble Indian, who had come so many times, wished to see him. He had already waited a long time. The bishop realized that this had to be the proof needed to certify and act on the humble Indian's request. He immediately ordered that he be admitted.

Upon entering, Juan Diego bowed humbly before the bishop as he had done before and retold the story of all that he had seen and wondered at and repeated the message: "My lord, I did what you commanded me. I went to tell my mistress, the heavenly Lady, holy Mary, the beloved Mother of God, that you asked her for a sign so that you might believe me that you are to build a chapel where she asks you to. I also told her that I had promised to bring you the sign and proof of her will that you asked me to bring. And she has well received the word of your breath. She was well pleased by your request for a sign and proof, so that her beloved will may be done. Very early today she commanded me to come see you again. I asked for the sign that would make you believe me that sign which she had promised to give me. She sent me to the top of the hill was not a place where flowers could grow, since it is a place of rocks, thistles, thorns, cactus and mesquite, but I did not doubt. As I approached the top of the hill I saw that I was in paradise, where there were exquisite Castilian roses, brilliant with dew, which I proceeded to cut. When I had cut them, I brought them down; she took them in her hands, rearranged them, and placed them in my tilma, so that I might bring them and give them to you in person. She told me that I must deliver them to you, as a sign of the truth of my world and my message to have her will be done. Here they are. Please receive them."

The he unfurled his white tilma in which he had folded the flowers. As the different Castilian roses scattered over the floor, there was suddenly imprinted, visibly, the wonderful image of the ever-virgin, holy Mary, Mother of God, as it is now preserved and on display in her chapel in Tepeyac, now called Guadalupe.

As soon as the bishop and others present saw it, they fell to their knees. They were overwhelmed with amazement and awe. They became sad, and their hearts and minds were in ecstasy. The bishop, crying tears of repentance, prayed and asked pardon for not having begun to carry out her will and command. Standing, he untied from Juan Diego's neck the tilma on which the heavenly Lady was made manifest. Then he took it and placed it in his chapel. The bishop asked him to stay, so Juan Diego remained one more day in the bishop's house. The next day the bishop said: "Now let us go see where the heavenly Lady wants her chapel built." And he immediately invited everyone who might be concerned with its construction to go along.

As soon as Juan Diego showed him where the heavenly Lady commanded that her chapel be raised, he asked permission to leave. He now wanted to go home to see his uncle Juan Bernardino, the one who was so sick that it had left him to go to Tlatelolco and call a priest to hear his confession and prepare him for death, the one whom the heavenly Lady had declared already cured. However, they would not let him go alone, but accompanied him to his home.

Arriving, they saw that his uncle was happy and free from pain. He was astonished that his nephew arrived in such a state, with so many people, and asked him why they did this and why they were showing him such respect. His nephew answered that when he left to call the priest to hear his confession and prepare him for death, the heavenly Lady had appeared to him on Tepeyac Hill, telling him not the be upset, that his uncle was cured, which greatly comforted him; she sent him to Mexico to see the bishop so that he would build her a house on Tepeyac Hill. The uncle revealed that he was sure that he was cured at that moment, and that he saw her at the same moment in the same image, as she appeared to his nephew. He had learned from her that she had sent his nephew to see the bishop in Mexico. The Lady also told him that when he should go to see the bishop, he should make known what he had seen and the miraculous way he had been cured and that the blessed image should always be called and she should be worshipped there as the ever-virgin holy Maria of Guadalupe.

They then took Juan Bernardino before the bishop to report and bear witness before him. When he and his nephew arrived together, the bishop offered them hospitality in his house for a few days, until a shrine to the Queen of Tepeyac could be built where she had appeared to Juan Diego. The bishop moved the holy image of the beloved heavenly Lady to the cathedral, taking it from the chapel in his palace, so that all the people could see and wonder at her blessed image. The whole city was deeply moved: they came to see and wonder at her revered image, whose divine origin they recognized, and pray to her. Many were astonished at the miraculous way she had appeared, for no person in this world had painted her beloved image.

Luis Lasso de la Vega, *Nican Mopohua*, Mexico City, 1649

Chapter 3
Our Lady of Laus

The Virgin Mary has had a special place in her heart for the country of France, as well as poor shepherd girls. King Louis XIII consecrated France to Mary in 1638, for many years France was the pivotal country in Europe. It was at the forefront in politics, intellectual activity, and social change.

In 1664, Benoite Rencurel was tending a flock of sheep. This was in the Laus Valley, near the town of Dauphine'. Benoite was seventeen years old at the time. An older man approached Benoite, dressed in clerical garments. He approached Benoite asked the man who he was. He replied, "I am Maurice, to who the nearby chapel is dedicated. "...My daughter, do not come back to this place. It is part of a different territory, and the shepherds would take your flock if they found it here. Go to the valley about Saint E'tienne. That is where you will see the Mother of God". Benoite responded that the Virgin Mary was in Heaven, not France. Maurice said, "Yes, she is in Heaven, and on earth too when She wants".

(It should be noted that the chapel Maurice referred to was in a ruined state)

Benoite lead her flock where Maurice indicated, the valley of Kilns. There she encountered a beautiful lady who was standing in a sort of grotto in the rock. Initially, Mary said nothing to Benoite, though the girl tried to engage Mary in conversation.

This visual exposure continued for an intermittent period of two months before verbal contact was made. A Mrs. Rolland, employer of Benoite, followed her to see who Benoite was visiting. Mrs. Rolland did see Mary. Mary then told Benoite to tell her employer to not take her Son's name in vain (swearing), or she would never see Heaven.

Mary finally admitted to Benoite who she was, saying: "I am Mary the mother of Jesus". She also told Benoite she would only see her in the chapel at Laus, from then on. This was an abandoned chapel in the neighboring village.

When Benoite made her journey to the chapel she immediately saw Mary. Mary asked Benoite to help in the building of a church, at the old chapel's site. Benoite said there was no money for the construction, but the Virgin Mary said the money would be raised.

News of the apparitions spread, with many pilgrimages to the abandoned chapel. There was, though, the almost immediate skepticism on the part of the local clergy. Especially antagonistic towards the apparitions was the Vicar General, Father Pierre Gaillard. The Virgin Mary told Benoite to relay to Father Gaillard the following: "Sire, although you command God each morning and make Him come down to the altar by the power you received when you became a priest, you have no commands to give to His Holy Mother, who does as she pleases here".

Father Galliard was impressed by the response from Benoite, but asked her to tell the Virgin that they needed to see a miracle to validate the apparition. This miracle, in the form of a healing to a long crippled woman, occurred almost immediately.

A church was built on the site of the chapel in October, 1666. This complied with the wishes of the Virgin Mary. Also, it is clear that the miraculous events requested by the clergy really happened.

Another feature of the Laus apparitions was what is called the "odor of sanctity". An incredible number of testimonies were collected that spoke of glorious fragrances around Benoit and the church, Judge Fracois Grimaud spoke of it, saying: "During the Easter season of 1666, I smelled a very sweet fragrance for around seven minutes; I had never smelled anything like it in my life, and it gave me such deep satisfaction that I was enraptured".

This phenomenon is extremely common, occurring to such notables as Catherine Labouré', and Saint Therese of Lisieux. I am certainly no saint, yet I experienced it myself. (see Conclusion) It is most certainly not a hallucination, and it is never expected. Also, the fragrance is so powerful and cloying it has a very supernatural feel to it. As in the above quote, the experience leaves the lucky recipient in a euphoric state.

Benoite enjoyed the company of the Virgin Mary for over fifty years, till her death in 1718. She also experienced an apparition of Jesus and many contacts with her guardian angel. She became a nun before her death, and died in the previously mentioned "odor of sanctity".

Benoite was beatified in 1984, the step just before being declared a saint of the church. In May 2008, the apparition of Laus was given the status of having a "supernatural nature". It is one of the few to have reached this high level of acceptance.

Benoite was a very humble, sweet individual-very much like Catherine Labouré and Bernadette Soubirous. The Virgin Mary is obviously attracted to innocent souls like these. God uses them as contact points with the rest of us.

Chapter 4
Rue Du Bac: The Miraculous Medal

Catherine Labouré was born into a large family in Fain-les-Moutiers, in the province of Burgundy, France. She was born on May 2, 1806, the feast day of St. Joe. It was because of this birth date that her nick name was Zoe. Her parents were Pierre and Madeleine. Her father was the most successful farmer in the region, and he was even mayor of the village at one time.

Burgundy, like other homes of seers, was a quiet farming province. Life was simple: farm work, family and church. This was the same province that produced St. Joan of Arc.

Catherine was raised in a devout Catholic home. Her father even considered the priesthood in his youth, before settling on farming. Her mother, Madeleine, installed a strong faith and conviction in all her children. Her older sister, Marie Louise, had early on decided to enter a convent when family circumstances allowed.

Catherine Labouré was every bit drawn to religious life as her older sister. Due to her mother's early death, Catherine had to fill in as surrogate head of household. Finally, in January of 1830, her father gave permission for her to enter the postulancy (convent) at Hospice de la Charite at Chatillon. This was part of the religious order of the Daughters of Charity.

April, 1830 saw Catherine transferred to what would become a famous location. She was sent to 140 Rue du Bac, Paris, the headquarters of the order.

Shortly after arriving at the Paris location, Sister Catherine had a vision that the French king would be over thrown. She related this to her confessor, Father Aladel. This would later prove to be an accurate prophecy, and it would also underscore the validity of Catherine's whole experience.

On the night of June 18, 1830, the apparitions began. As Catherine was sleeping, a voice called out to her. She pulled aside her sleeping curtain, and saw a small child in a white robe. The child (angel) was holding a candle, and asked Catherine to follow him. (Note: Many reported sightings of angels describe them as having the appearance of young children)

The angel said that the Blessed Virgin was waiting to see her. They went through the dormitory, past the sleeping nuns, towards the chapel. The chapel was all ablaze with candles, like during a Christmas service.

The angel then said, "Here is the Blessed Virgin". Catherine heard a sound of rustling like silk, and saw a beautiful lady sit in the chair Father Aladel used for services.

The Virgin Mary began her message to Catherine saying, "My child, the good God wishes to charge you with a mission. You will be tormented until you have told him who is directing you (Father Aladel)...Tell with confidence all that passes within you. Tell it simply. Do not be afraid.

But come now to the foot of the altar. There graces will be shed on all, great or small, who fervently ask for them. There will be great danger for this seminary, and other religious communities. At one moment when the danger is acute, everyone will believe all to be lost; you will recall my visit and this seminary will have the protection of God. But it will not be the same for all religious communities."

A sadness the came over Mary as she continued, "Among the clergy there will be victims, Monsignor the Archbishop, my child, the cross will be treated with contempt, they will hurl it to the ground and trample it. Blood will flow. The streets will run with blood. Monsignor the Archbishop will be stripped of his garments. My eyes will ever be upon you. I shall grant you graces. Special graces will be given to all who ask them, but people must pray".

Catherine knew instinctively that some of these predictions were immediate, and some would take place forty years in the future. Catherine told Father Aladel, and the seminary director, about the apparitions and their content. Unlike other examples, an order of secrecy was given to her about the visions.

King Charles was deposed only eight days after the first apparition. This, of course, raised the credibility of Catherine's testimony. In addition, the civil unrest and forcible stripping of the Archbishop also came to pass. Nothing, as Mary indicated, would harm Catherine's seminary.

The next apparition came four months later, on November 27, 1830. Here is Catherine's account:

"On November 27, 1830, this fell on the Saturday before the first Sunday of advent, at five-thirty in the evening...I heard a sound like the rustling of a silk dress, from the tribune near the picture of St. Joseph.

Turning in that direction, I saw the Blessed Virgin Mary at the level of the picture. The Virgin was standing, she was of medium height, and clothed all in white. Her dress was of the whiteness of the dawn, made in the style called "a la vierge" that is, high neck and plain sleeves. A white veil covered her head and fell (to) either side of her feet. Under the veil her hair, in coils, was bound with a fillet ornamented with lace. Her face was sufficiently exposed, indeed exposed very well, and so beautiful that it seemed to me impossible to express her ravishing beauty.

Her feet rested on a white globe that is to say, half glove, or at least I only saw half. There was also a serpent, green in color with yellow spots.

A frame, slightly oval in shape, formed around the Blessed Virgin. Within it was written in letters of gold: "O Mary, conceived without sin, pray for us who have recourse to thee"

The inscription, in a semi-circle, began at the height of the right hand, passed over the head, and finishing at the height of the left hand. The hands were raised to the height of the stomach and held, in a very relaxed manner as if offering it to God. A golden ball surmounted with a little golden cross, which represented to the

43

world. Her eyes were not raised to heaven, now lowered. Her face was of such beauty I could not describe it.

All at once I saw rings on her fingers, three rings to each finger, the largest one near the base of the finger, one of medium size in the middle, the smallest one at the tip. Each ring was set, with gems, some more beautiful than others. The larger gems emitted greater rays and the smaller gems, smaller rays; the rays bursting from all sides flooded the base, so that I could no longer see the feet of the Blessed Virgin.

At this moment, while I was contemplating her the Blessed Virgin lowered her eyes and looked at me. I heard a voice speaking these words: "This ball that you see represents the whole world, especially France, and each person in particular." I could not express what I felt at this, what I saw, the beauty and the brilliance of the dazzling rays. "They are the symbols of the graces I shed upon those who asked for them. The gems from which rays do not fall are the graces which souls forget to ask."

The golden ball disappeared in the brilliance of the sheaves of light bursting from all sides; the hands turned out and the arms were bent down under the weight of treasures of grace obtained.

Then the voice said, "Have a medal struck after this model. All who wear it will receive great graces; they should wear it around the neck. Graces will abound for those who wear it with confidence".

At this instant the tableau seemed to me to turn, and I beheld the reverse of the medal: A large M surmounted by a bar and cross; beneath the M were the hearts of Jesus and Mary, the one crowned with thorns, the other pierced with a sword." At this point, the apparition ended.

There were several further apparitions of the Virgin to Catherine. Even after the physical apparitions ended, Catherine could hear the Virgin Mary's voice in her prayers for the rest of her life.

The archbishop, at the prompting of Father Aladel, began producing the Miraculous Medal in large quantities. This was in accordance with the wishes of the Blessed Virgin. Miraculous cures have been reported by the thousands over the years. There have been literally millions of medals distributed since the 1830's.

One interesting, and well authenticated, account of a conversion experience occurred to a Jewish aristocrat by the name of Alphonse Ratisbonne. This individual, born in 1814 at Strasbourg, France, was a powerful anti-Catholic. In his own words, Ratisbonne said, "I cherished hatred against priests, churches and convents, and especially against the Jesuits, whose very name goaded me to frenzy".

Upon a visit to Rome, his friend Baron Theodore de Bussieres, a fervent Catholic, prevailed upon Ratisbonne to wear the Miraculous Medal. To placate his friend, Alphonse wore the medal, and recited the Catholic prayer Memorare.

The following day, January 20, 1842, Ratisbonne accompanied the Baron to a funeral at the Basilica of St. Andrea Delle Fratte. As Ratisbonne wandered on his own, he saw an apparition of the Virgin. He, of course, was awestruck and immediately fell to his knees. He cried out, "How happy I am! How good God is! How unbelievers are to be pitied!"

This apparition and resulting conversion caused uproar in Europe. Ratisbonne converted to Catholicism, and broke off his engagement to be married. Eventually, he even became a priest.

Catherine Labouré died in 1876, after a long and dedicated career as a Daughter of Charity nun. She was declared a saint in 1947. Just previous to this, in 1933, her body was exhumed. Like Bernadette Soubirous, Catherine's body was found incorrupt, still flexible and not decayed after all those years.

Chapter 5
Our Lady of La Salette

The town of Corps is located in the French Alps, about 50 miles from Grenoble. Nothing really distinguished Corps from other small towns in the region. Lourdes was a very strategic location in French history, but poor Corps was famous only for the apparition of the Virgin Mary in September of 1846.

Maximin Giraud was the eleven year old son of the local wheelwright. He was not a great student, and was also somewhat of a free spirit. Though he came from a religious household, Maximin was not overly drawn to religion.

A local farmer was in need of help in shepherding his cows, and approached Maximin's father about hiring the boy for temporary employment. Terms were agreed upon, so Maximin and his faithful dog Lou Lou were now shepherds. This work was to be done in the neighboring town of Ablandins, parish of La Salette.

On September 14, 1846, Maximin set out for Ablandins to work for the term of one week. On his journey, he ran into another young shepherd by the name of Melanie Mathieu. She was fourteen years old, and a real full-time herder. Her family was large, so Melanie was hired out nine months a year to tend flocks of various farmers.

The two children had spent the better part of a day together when events started to occur. Melanie was the first to notice something strange when she crested the hill. She called for Maximin. She saw a strange, and powerful glowing light in the valley below them. It was in the form of a globe, and seemed to open. A beautiful woman was seen in the middle of this light, and was bent forward. Her elbows were resting on her knees, and she was crying.

Now the woman rose to a standing position. Her beauty was striking. She wore a long white dress, crossed by a shawl. On this shawl was embroidery of roses. She wore an apron that was gold in color. In the center of the dress was a large cross. On the left side of the crucifix was a hammer, and the right side had a pair of pliers. These were, of course, tools used in the crucifixion. The beautiful lady wore a large crown, also adorned with roses.

The beautiful lady asked the children if they said their prayers, the children responding, only a little. She then asked them if they had ever seen spoiled wheat. Maximin said he never had, but the Virgin Mary reminded him of a time with his father when he did see grain like that.

The Blessed Mother warned the children that the crops would fail, and famine would sweep the land. There was a ray of hope offered. If people would turn back to God, the worst suffering and disease could be avoided.

She said specifically, "If you have grain, it will do no good to sow it, for what you sow the beast will ear, and whatever part of it springs up will crumble into dust when you thresh it. A great famine is coming. But before that happens, the children under seven years of age will be seized with trembling and die the arms of parents holding them. The grownups will pay for their sins by hunger. The grapes will rot and the walnuts will turn bad. I f people are converted, the rock will become piles of wheat and it will be found the potatoes have sown themselves.

Only a few rather old women got to mass in the summer. Everyone else works every Sunday, all summer long. And in winter, when they don't know what to do with themselves, they go to mass only to scoff at religion. During Lent, they go to butcher shops like dogs".

The Virgin Mary said: "Well, my children, you will make this known to all my people". The children noticed that the lady did not actually walk on the grass, but she basically glided over it! At this point, the Virgin faded away from view.

The children were obviously awestruck by this experience. They went home and told their parents of the events. They were, of course, skeptical. The children were grilled endlessly, even by the mayor of the town. They were threatened, as seers usually are by the investigative authorities. But, these little seers kept to their story, and seemed quite truthful.

A side note to the story emerged. Upon investigating the apparitional site it was found that there was a flowing stream that had never been seen before. Remember, all the grazing areas, and water sources, were well know in this solely agricultural area.

The water was found to have healing qualities, similar to Lourdes. Many miraculous healings were attributed to the stream's water. The prophecies of crop failures came to pass, which gave great credibility to the testimony of the two children.

Finally, after five years of fulfilled prophecy, and impressive cures, Bishop Brulliard released these findings:

"Five years ago we were told of an event most extraordinary and, at first hearing, unbelievable, as having occurred on one of the mountains in our diocese. I was a matter of nothing less than an apparition of the Blessed virgin, who was said to have been seen by two herders on September 19, 1846. She told them of evils threatening her people, especially because of blasphemy and the profanation of Sunday, and she confided to each a particular secret, forbidding that these be communicated to anyone.

"In spite of the natural candor of the two herders; in spite of the impossibility of collusion by two ignorant children who hardly knew each other; in spite of the constancy and firmness of their witness which has never varied either when confronted by the agents of the law or by thousands of person who have exhausted every trick to involve them in contradiction or wrest their secrets from them, it has been our duty to refrain for a long time from accepting an event which seemed to us so marvelous.

"Haste on our part would not only have been contrary to the prudence which the great Apostle recommends to a bishop; it would also have served to buttress the prejudices of the enemies of our religion and of a grant many Catholics who are Catholics only in name. While a multitude of pious souls warmly welcomed this reputed apparition as a fact, we again and again considered with care all the grounds which could lead us to reject it. Hence we have braved until now the criticisms which we well know have been directed at us by people, with the best of intentions in other respects, who accuse us, perhaps, of indifference or even of stark lack of faith.

"On the other hand, we were strictly obliged not to regard as impossible an event which the Lord (who would dare deny it?) might well have permitted to further His glory, for His arm is not shortened and His power is the same today as in ages past.

"While our Episcopal duty imposed on us the necessity of waiting, pondering, fervently begging the light of the Holy Spirit, the number of wonders noised about on all sides was constantly growing. There was word of unusual cures worked in different parts of France and in other places, even countries far away. Sick people in desperate straits, either given up by their doctors as certain to die soon or condemned to long drawn out suffering, have been reported restored to perfect health after invocation of Our Lady of La Salette and the use, with faith, of water from a spring at which the Queen of Heaven appeared to the two herders.

"From the very first days, people have spoken to us of this spring. We have been assured that it had never before flowed steadily, but gave water only after snows or heavy rains. It was dry that September 19; thereafter it began to flow and has flowed constantly ever since: marvelous water, if not in its origin, at least in its effects."

The bishop treated other features of La Salette, one by one, and outlined the process of investigation and discussion carried on at his insistence. He alluded to his consultation with other bishops, their sharing his view that this was indisputably a prodigy, their being convinced that cures of people in their respective dioceses were miraculous, their allowing public preaching about the apparition and the placing of statues of Our Lady of La Salette in parish churches. Then came the formal declaration:

"Conforming to the principles laid down by Pope Benedict XIV, and following the path traced by him in his immortal work, *On the Beatification and the Canonization of Saints*, Book II, Chapter XXI, Number 12;

"Having read the account written by Father Rousselot, one of our vicars general, and published under the title *The Truth Concerning the Event of La Salette* (Grenoble, 1848);

"Having also read *New Documents Concerning the Event of La Salette*, published by the same author in 1850, both of these works invested with our approbation;

"Having heard the discussions, representing different opinions, which took place in our presence in sessions on November 8, 15, 16, 17, 22, 29 and December 6 and 23, 1847;

"Likewise having read or heard what has, since that time, been written or said for or against the Event;

"Considering, in the first place, the impossibility of explaining the fact of
La Salette in any other way than by divine intervention, whether it is looked at in itself, in its circumstances, or in its essentially religious aim;

"Considering, in the second place, that the marvelous consequences of the fact of La Salette are the witness of God Himself, manifesting Himself by miracles, and that this witness is superior to that of men and their objections;

"Considering that these two grounds, taken separately or, much more together, ought to dominate the whole question and deprive of every trace of validity those contrary pretensions or suppositions of which we declare that we are fully aware;

"Considering, finally, that obedience and submission to heaven's warnings can spare us the new chastisements with which we are threatened, while too long resistance can lay us open to evils beyond repair;

"On the express demand of all the members of our venerable chapter of canons and of the overwhelming majority of the priests of our diocese;

"Having invoked afresh the Holy Spirit and the assistance of the Immaculate Virgin;

"We declare the following:

"1. We give judgment that the apparition of the Blessed virgin to two herders on September 19, 1846, on the mountain of the Alpine chain situated in the parish of La Salette, in the territory of the archpriest of Corps, bears in itself all the marks of truth, and the faithful have grounds to believe it indubitable and certain.

"2. We believe that this event acquires a further degree of certitude from the immense and spontaneous flocking of the faithful to the scene of the apparition, as well as from the abundance of marvels which have come in the wake of this event and a very great number of which cannot be called in doubt without violating the rules of human testimony.

"3. Therefore, to demonstrate our lively thanks to God and to the glorious Virgin Mary, we authorize the cult of Our Lady of La Salette.

"Given at Grenoble September 19, 1851, the fifth anniversary of the famous apparition.

"Philibert, Bishop of Grenoble."

Chapter 6
Our Lady of Lourdes

Lourdes is a small village in the southwestern region of France. It is in the foothills of the Pyrenees Mountains, bordering France and Spain. The actual border lies only 26 miles from the town.

It has an ancient fort that was built by no less than Julius Caesar, in the Gallic Wars. Lourdes was a strategic point for hundreds of years after the Romans. The Muslim Saracens occupied it for a time, till they were defeated by Charlemagne in 778. Various factions still struggled for control of the fort till France unified under monarchial control. The fort remained a military post till 1894 when it was turned into a museum.

The area surrounding the village is one of great natural beauty, with majestic mountain views. Rivers also run their course through the region, enhancing its appeal.

It was in this setting that Bernadette Soubirous was born on January 7, 1844. Her parents were Francois and Louise Soubirous who originally were operators of a leased mill.

Unfortunately, Bernadette's parents fell on extremely hard times. They lost the lease on the original mill in 1855. In spite of attempts of trying to rebuild their financial circumstances, the family seemed on a continual downward spiral. This continued till they had to take up accommodations at what at one time was the town jail. This dank dwelling measured only 16 X 13 feet. Needless to say, Bernadette's childhood was very difficult, probably resulting in the poor health which followed her most of her life.

Bernadette's schooling was spotty at best. She attended for a time, but was soon pressed into duty as a shepherd. (Note: This is a striking similarity to the seers at Fatima.) Bernadette tired of the surroundings and made her way back to Lourdes.

On February 11, 1858, Bernadette, her sister Toinette, and friend Jeannie Abadie were gathering wood for the family's fireplace. The three girls ventured quite a way from their residence, roughly half a mile. They followed the mill stream till it ended, at a point called Massabielle. This was a hill of about 100 feet in height.

At the base of this hill was a grotto, about thirty-nine feet across and thirty feet deep. This was to be the site of the apparitions of the Virgin Mary.

The girls became separated, with Bernadette at the grotto. Toinette and Jeannie had gone to the other side of the stream. Bernadette noticed a glowing light that surrounded a young girl; who seemed to be hovering over a wild rose bush. The young girl motioned for Bernadette to come forward.

Bernadette became scared, taking out her rosary for protection. Mary, hovering over the rose bush, did the same thing. After Bernadette completed the sequence of prayers, the young girl again motioned for Bernadette to come closer. She didn't respond, Mary smiled and started to disappear. The light remained for a few additional moments, and then it also faded.

The other two girls returned, finding Bernadette pale and unresponsive to their questions. Slowly, Bernadette returned from her daze, and the girls returned home.

The account of the grotto experience soon swept through the town. Bernadette was harshly treated by her parents for basically making up fanciful stories.

Three days later, on February 14, Bernadette, along with several other girls, returned to the grotto. Bernadette was carrying a vial of holy water for protection. Bernadette started saying the Rosary again, and another vision occurred. Only Bernadette could see the Virgin Mary. Her companions could only see Bernadette talking to a point in front and above her.

After the vision, Bernadette seemed lost again in a world of her own, and very pale. Her companions were frightened and they enlisted the help of a neighbor to carry Bernadette home. Her parents decided to forbid further trips to the grotto initially.

Their mind was changed by two prominent local women who wanted to accompany Bernadette to the grotto. The group returned on February 18th. Another vision ensued, with Bernadette asking Mary to write down what she wanted. The Virgin said it was not necessary. She also told Bernadette she could not make her happy in this world, but she could in the next. She also asked Bernadette to return for the next 14 days.

The next apparitional event was witnessed by a large crowd, including Bernadette's mother. Bernadette was the only witness to the apparition, and again, she went into an "ecstasy" where she was totally absorbed by the vision.

Though it was clear to almost everyone who had heard of the apparitions, the visitor still had not formally identified herself. Bernadette referred to her as "the lady".

This lady was described as wearing a beautiful gown of glowing white with blue accents. In her hands was a golden rosary. The physical appearance was of a young girl, yet exuding enormous power. Her instruction to Bernadette was to "pray to God for sinners".

The local district attorney, as well as other local officials, began meeting to put a stop to the goings on at the grotto. This is the usual response to apparitions at first. Lourdes was no exception. Both the local district attorney and police superintendent "grilled" Bernadette. Both were grudgingly convinced of the young girl's sincerity.

The seventh apparition was when the world famous healing waters of Lourdes were discovered. The Virgin Mary directed Bernadette where to start digging with her hand. She dug briefly in the sand of the grotto and produced a small trickle of water at first. Within hours, the trickle of water grew greatly in intensity.

The Virgin Mary also told Bernadette to ask the local priest to have a chapel built on this site. It was at this point the little seer was exposed to even more skepticism, this time by the clergy. The local priest insisted that he needed identification from this "visitor". Bernadette said she would formally ask at the next meeting.

At the next apparitional meeting, Bernadette posed the priest's question to the heavenly visitor. Mary's reply was, "I am the Immaculate Conception!" This was the identity that separated the "visitor" from the merely angelic realm.

There were, in all, eighteen apparitions of the Virgin Mary at Lourdes. After examining Bernadette exhaustively, and compiling data on the incredible number of miraculous healings from the water of Lourdes, a finding was made in 1862 on the validity of Lourdes.

The bishop of Tarbes declared, upon investigation:

Article 1. We adjudge that the Immaculate Mary, Mother of God, really appeared to Bernadette Soubirous on February 11, 1858, and subsequent days, eighteen times in all, in the grotto of Massabielle, near the town of Lourdes: that this apparition possesses all the marks of the truth, and that the faithful are justified in believing it certain. We humbly submit our judgment to the judgment of the supreme Pontiff to whom is committed the government of the whole church.

Article 2. We authorize in our diocese the cult of Our Lady of Lourdes...

Article 3. In conformity with the will of the Blessed Virgin, which was made known on several occasions during the apparition, we propose to build a sanctuary on the terrain of the grotto, which has become the property of the Bishop of Tarbes.

To re-cap, the key points of Bernadette's apparitional experience:

1. Bernadette, with a meager education at this point, could not possibly have known of the Catholic doctrine of the "Immaculate Conception". This doctrine is one that says the Virgin Mary, like Jesus, also was born without sin. Bernadette admitted upon interrogation that she had no idea of the meaning of this term.

2. During various instances of religious "ecstasy", the young seer was oblivious to pain and her surroundings. Doctors checked her pulse and blood pressure, noting no change relative to pain. The consensus was that no one could fake this condition under duress.

3. The element of the healing waters of Lourdes must be considered. Bernadette uncovered, with Mary's direction, a stream in the grotto. It started with a small trickle, and grew to 25,000 gallons a day within 24 hours.

   The volume, though remarkable, is not the most fascinating aspect about Lourdes water. Thousands have reported miraculous cures over the years. Many of these have been investigated by doctors with no natural explanation. Over fifteen million visit the shrine, with its healing waters, every year.

Bernadette Soubirous entered religious life after the apparitions. She was sixteen when the mayor of Lourdes got her admitted to the school of the Sisters of Nevers. She was a member of this order till her death in 1879, at the age of thirty-two.

Bernadette's body was exhumed in 1919, and found "incorrupt". Her body is in a glass case for viewing at the orders chapel in Nevers, France. One can view her body on the internet, in its pristine condition. She was canonized as a saint in 1933.

Bernadette was the only one who saw Mary during the apparitions, yet miraculous "proofs" exist to prove the truth of her claims. It is possible this little seer may be considered the most famous of them all.

Chapter 7
Our Lady of Pontmain

The Virgin Mary has an affinity for remote, agricultural areas. Though Zeitoun was witnessed by millions in crowded Cairo, rural locations are definitely the preference. Further, for some unexplained reason, the country of France is a preferred location as well. France has always been a heavily Catholic country. Unfortunately, France has also been the focal point for just about every European war.

The year 1871 saw a political situation that was repeated often. Germany was invading France, with devastating results for the French. Napoleon III was trying to recapture the military glory of his grandfather, Napoleon I. Otto Von Bismarck was the new German chancellor, having succeeded in uniting all the small Germanic states.

The small village of Pontmain is located in the northwest corner of the country, on the boundary between Brittany and Normandy. It was a non-descript town with no particular claim to fame. The only notable born in the area was the great Catholic Saint Therese of Lisieux.

On January 17, 1871, the Germans had advanced to Laval, the closest town to Pontmain. All the Germans had to do was cross the Mayenne River to complete the capture of Laval. At this same time, the local bishop appealed to the Virgin Mary for her intercession. He asked her to spare the city, and end the hostilities. At the same time, very dramatic events were ready to unfold in Pontmain.

Caesar Barbadette was in his Pontmain barn with Eugene, age 12, and Joseph, age 12. The three were finishing up their chores before the evening meal. This particular family was a very devout Catholic one. Mass was regularly attended, and prayers were said daily. Their general reputation was very solid and respectable.

Eugene Barbadette looked over to the house of Augustine Guidecoq. Hovering a few feet over the roof was a beautiful woman. She wore a black veil and had a gold crown on her head. Further, she was smiling in his direction. Eugene was transfixed at this site for some 10 to 15 minutes. An older neighbor came by, but she could not see the lady.

The father and younger brother Joseph joined the two. Only Joseph could see the "tall lady". He described her as wearing a blue dress with gold stars. Joseph also indicated she wore a crown with a red band around it. She had her arms extended, as in the figure on the Miraculous Medal. Caesar Barbadette could see nothing, and told his boys it was time to go back to the house for dinner.

Caesar hesitated before they left the barn. He knew his sons were truthful and not prone to flights of fancy. He asked Eugene to go back and see if the vision was still there. Eugene looked out, and confirmed the lady was still hovering over the neighbors' house. Caesar sent the boy to fetch the mother, Victoria, for consultation. As with the father, Victoria could not see the lady either. Both parents now became frustrated with the sons, and ordered everyone to the house for dinner.

After dinner, Victoria sent the two boys out to verify their vision. They did confirm the continual presence of the "lady", and also indicated she was quite tall. Eugene and Joseph compared her to Sister Vitaline, a local nun.

The family went to the local school to enlist the help and advice of Sister Vitaline. She came back to the house, but she couldn't see the Virgin Mary. She did, however, see an unusual formation of three stars. This was what the seers said were directly over the lady's head.

The sister then sent for three borders at the local school, Frances Richer, Jeanne Marie Labosse, and another child. The first two girls could see the Virgin Mary; while the unidentified child could not. This was enough confirmation for Sister Vitaline to send for the local priest, Father Guerin.

As father Guerin arrived, Sister Vitaline was leading the assembly in the "Red Rosary". This was a short devotion to a group of Japanese martyrs who were killed shortly before the apparition.

Father Guerin took control over the scene, and it was quickly determined that only the little children could see the Virgin. This correlated with most Marian apparitions. Children, presumably for their innocence, are the seers of choice. (Note: There are notable exceptions to this preference. Examples include Guadalupe, Akita, and Zeitoun, among others).

The descriptions collected from the children were of an animated Mary. Her features reacted to the mood of the crowd, and the stars on her garment began multiplying. The increase in stars corresponded to the repetition of the Rosary prayers.

One of the nuns, Sister Marie Edward, began the saying of the Magnificat, a Marian prayer derived from the gospel of Luke. As this prayer was sung, another change occurred with the apparition. A banner unrolled at the lady's feet, with the French words, "Maiz Priez, Mes Enfants". The English translation is, "But pray my children."

It was discussed in the crowd that a prayer should be said for deliverance from the invading Germans. The words then formed on the banner: "Dieu, vous exaucera en peu de temp". In English it meant, "God will hear you in a little while". This caused great feelings of relief and joy among the crowd, especially because thirty-eight men had been drafted into the French army.

Another message formed on the banner at Mary's feet. This message read: "Mon fils se laisse toucher". The translation in English is: "My Son allows Himself to be moved by compassion".

The entire crowd then began the singing of an old hymn, "Mother of Hope". This hymn held great and historic meaning for the French people. Thinking of Mary as our "Mother of Hope" had been in place for over 1,000 years. The children relayed that Mary smiled greatly at the reciting of the hymn.

A large crucifix appeared in the lady's hands. This was held forwards toward the crowd, with the implied meaning that the French should put their confidence in Jesus.

Father Guerin had the crowd begin the evening prayer ritual that prevailed in that area. It was while these prayers were being recited that the children saw a white veil begin to cover up the Virgin's figure. The veil rose from her feet towards her face. The veils progress halted for a moment as she smiled. Then, Mary was gone. The entire period of observation lasted three hours.

The German Army did not occupy Laval, as was expected. News had reached the Germans, also Catholics, that the Blessed Virgin Mary was protecting this area. Within a few days, peace was declared. The war came to an end with the Virgins' promise being fulfilled. She said, "My Son allows himself to be touched".

The church launched a complete investigation into the events at Pontmain. The local bishop, Wicart, put on Father Vincent in charge of the proceedings.

After much grilling and threatening, the bishop was convinced the children were telling the truth. Their stories were consistent in details, not rehearsed. It was even found that the children were not influenced by previous apparitions at Lourdes or La Salette.

The bishop issued the following statement after the proceedings: "We judge that the Immaculate Virgin Mother of God, truly appeared January 17, 1871 to Eugene Barbadette, Joseph Barbadette, Frances Richer and Jeanne Marie Labosse in the hamlet of Pontmain.

"We submit this judgment, in all humility and obedience to the supreme judgment of the Holy Apostolic see, center of unity and organ of truth in the whole church".

It was mentioned earlier that the local people sang a hymn referring to Mary as Our Lady of Hope. This was the title that the bishop applied to this apparition.

Their hopes and prayers were answered, just as the Virgin Mary said they would be. Coincidence the German advance stopped right outside Laval? Probably not.

Chapter 8
Our Lady of Knock

It's hard to believe in the current era of vast St. Patrick's Day parades and festivals, that being Irish used to be very undesirable. Even my own Irish roots were covered up so we could pass as English.

The Irish potato famine of the 1850's devastated this poor country. Without advanced technology, they could do little but starve or leave. And leave they did, starting an exodus that went on for decades.

The scene for this apparition occurred on August 21, 1879. The town was the village of Knock, county Mayo. It was against this gloomy backdrop of poverty, in a rustic backwater, that the Virgin Mary made her appearance.

Archdeacon Cavanaugh, the local priest, had a housekeeper by the name of Mary McLoughlin. Here is her testimony, as the initial witness to the events to the ecclesiastical commission:

"I, Mary McLoughlin," recorded the witness "live in Knock. I am a housekeeper to the Reverend Archdeacon Cavanagh; I remember the evening of the twenty-first August; at the hour of seven or so; or a little later, I passed from the Reverend Archdeacon's house on by the chapel, towards the house of a Mrs. Beirne, widow.

"On passing by the chapel, and at a little distance from it, I saw a wonderful number of strange figures or appearances at the gable; one like the Blessed Virgin Mary, and one like St. Joseph; another a bishop; I saw an altar; I was wondering to see there such an extraordinary group; yet I passed on and said nothing thinking that possibly the Archdeacon had been supplied with these beautiful figures from Dublin or somewhere else, and that he said nothing about them, but had left them in the open air; I saw a white light about them; I thought the whole thing strange.

"After looking at them, I passed on to the house of Mrs. Beirne in the village; after reaching widow Berine's house I stayed there half an hour at least; I returned then homewards to the Archdeacon's house accompanied by Miss Mary Beirne, and as we approached the chapel she cried out, 'Look at the beautiful figures'."

"We gazed at them for a little, and then I told her to go for her mother, widow Beirne, and her brother, and her sister, and her niece, who were still in the house which she and I had left. I remained looking at the sight before me until the mother, sister and brother of Mary Beirne came; at the time I was outside the ditch and to the southwest of the school house near the road, about thirty yards or so from the church; I leaned across the wall in order to see, as well as I could, the whole scene."

"I remained now for the space of at least a quarter of an hour, perhaps longer; I told Miss Beirne then to go for her uncle, Brian Beirne, and her aunt, Mrs. Bryan Beirne, or any of the neighbors whom she could see, in order that they might witness the sight that they (the witnesses) were then enjoying."

"I was now about a quarter past eight o'clock, and beginning to be quite dark. The sun had set; it was raining at the time. I beheld, on this occasion, not only the three figures, but an altar further on to the left of the figure of the Blessed Virgin Mary, and to the left of the bishop and above the altar a lamb about the size of that which is five weeks old. Behind the lamb appeared the cross; it was away a bit from the lamb, while the latter stood in front from it, and not resting on the wood of the cross. Around the lamb a number of gold-like stars appeared in the form of a halo. This altar was placed right under the window of the gable and more to the east of the figures, all, of course, outside the church at Knock."

"I parted from the company or gathering at eight and a half o'clock. I went to the priest's house and told what I had beheld, and spoke of the beautiful things that were to be seen at the gable of the chapel. I ask him or said, rather, it would be worth his while to go to witness them. He appeared to make nothing of what I said, and consequently he did not go."

"Although it was pouring rain the wall had a bright, dry appearance, while the rest of the building appeared to be dark. I did not return to behold the visions again after that, remaining at my house. I saw the sight for fully an hour."

"Very Reverend B. Cavanagh heard the next day all about the apparition from the others who had beheld it; and then it came to his recollection that I had told him the previous evening about it, and asked him to see it."

In addition to Mary McLoughlin's testimony, here is the testimony of fourteen year old Patrick Hill:

"I am Patrick Hill; I live in Claremorris; my aunt lives at Knock; I remember the twenty-first August last; on that day I was drawing home turf or peat from the bog, on an ass. While at my aunt's, at about eight o'clock in the evening, Dominick Beirne came into the house; he cried out: 'Come up to the chapel and see the miraculous lights, and the beautiful visions that are to be seen there.' I followed him; another man by name Dominick Beirne, and John Durkan, and a small boy named John Curry, came with me; we were all together; we ran towards the chapel. When we, running southwest, came so far from the village that on our turning the gable came into view, we immediately beheld the lights; a clear white light, covering most of the gable, from the ground up to the window and higher. It was a kind of changing bright light, going sometimes up high and again not so high. We saw the figures-the Blessed Virgin, St. Joseph, and St. John, and an altar with a lamb on the altar, and a cross behind the lamb."

At this time we reached as far as the wall fronting the gable; there were other people there before me; some of them were praying, some not; all were looking at the vision; they were leaning over the wall or ditch, with their arms resting on top. I saw the figures and the brightness; the boy, John Curry, from behind the wall did not see them, but I did; and he asked me to lift him up till he could see the grand babies, as the call the figures; it was raining; some, among them Mary McLoughlin, who beheld what I now saw, had gone away; others were coming."

After we prayed awhile I thought it right to go across the wall and into the chapel yard. I brought little Curry with me; I then went up closer; I saw everything distinctly. The figures were full and round as if they had a body and life; they said nothing; but as we approached they seemed to go back a little towards the gable. I distinctly beheld the Blessed Virgin Mary, life size, standing about two feet or so above the ground clothed in white robes which were fastened at the neck; her hands were raised to the height of the shoulders, as if in prayer, with the palms facing one another, but slanting towards the face; the palms were not turned towards the people, but facing each other as I have described; she appeared to be praying; her eyes were turned as I saw towards heaven; she wore a brilliant crown on her head and over the forehead where the crown fitted the brow, a beautiful rose; the crown appeared brilliant, and of a golden brightness, of a deeper hue, inclined to a mellow yellow, than the striking whiteness of the robes she wore; the upper part of the crown appeared to be a series of sparkles, or glittering crosses; I saw her eyes, the balls, the pupils and the iris of each. I noticed her hands especially, and face, her appearance! The robes came only as far as the ankles; I saw the feet and the ankles; on foot, the right, was slightly advanced of the other; at times she appeared, and all the figures appeared to move; she did not speak; I went up very near."

"One old woman went up and embraced the Virgin's feet, and she found nothing in her arms or hands; they receded, she said, from her."

"I saw St. Joseph to the Blessed Virgin's right hand; his head was bent, from the shoulders, forward; he appeared to be paying his respects; I noticed his whiskers; they appeared slightly gray; there was a line or dark smearing between the figure of the

Blessed Virgin and the spot where she stood. I saw the feet of St. Joseph, too. His hands were joined like a person at prayer."

"The third figure that stood before me was that of St. John the Evangelist. He stood erect at the Gospel side of the altar, and at an angle with the figure of the Blessed Virgin, so that his back was not turned to the altar, nor to the Mother of God. His right arm was at as angle with a line drawn across from St. Joseph to where Our Blessed Lady appeared to be standing; St. John was dressed like a bishop preaching; he wore a small mitre on his head; he held a Mass Book, or a Book of Gospels, in his left hand; the right hand was raised to the elevation of the head; while he kept the index finger and the middle finger of the right hand raised, the other three fingers of the same hand were shut; he appeared as if he were preaching, but I heard no voice; I came so near, that I looked into the book; I saw the lines and the letters. St. John wore no sandals, his left hand was turned towards the altar was behind him; the altar was a plain one, like any ordinary altar, without ornaments."

"One the altar stood a lamb, the size of a lamb of eight weeks old-the face of the lamb was fronting the west, and looking in the direction of the Blessed Virgin and St. Joseph; behind the lamb a large cross was placed erect or perpendicular on the altar; around the lamb I saw angels hovering during the whole time, for the space of one hour and a half or longer; I saw their wings fluttering, but I did not perceive their heads or faces, which were not turned to me."

"For the space of an hour and a half we were under the pouring rain; at this time I was very wet; I noticed that the rain did not wet the figures which appeared before me, although I was wet myself. I went away then."

There were fifteen witnesses that testified at the official church inquiry, held a few months after the event. The witnesses all corroborated each other's testimony, without deviation. It should be noted that there were over two hundred witnesses to the event.

Unlike other apparitions, the Virgin Mary did not speak. Also, she was seen by all involved, not just children. Frequently, she comes with a title like, "Our Lady of the Rosary" or "The Immaculate Conception". In this case, she was there to reassure the Irish that they were loved, and not forgotten.

Over the years, Archdeacon Cavanaugh maintained a diary of cures obtained by a pilgrimage to Knock. Numerous ones have been acclaimed as being miraculous in nature, i.e. the cures were way outside the realm of regular medical experience.

I have been in contact with the shrine of "Our Lady of Knock". They assure me at the shrine that the cures still continue and that they have a medical board that investigates them. A photo has been received from the shrine, showing numerous crutches that have been left from those experiencing such a cure.

Pope John Paul II made a visit to "Our Lady of Knock". This visit, as in other cases, effectively gave the events at Knock official church approval.

Photos

This photo was taken at the Shrine of Knock. Note all the crutches hanging in this photo. There were numerous miracles of healing in Knock.
Courtesy: Knock Museum

Bernadette, 1863, 19 years old.

Bernadette at Lourdes.

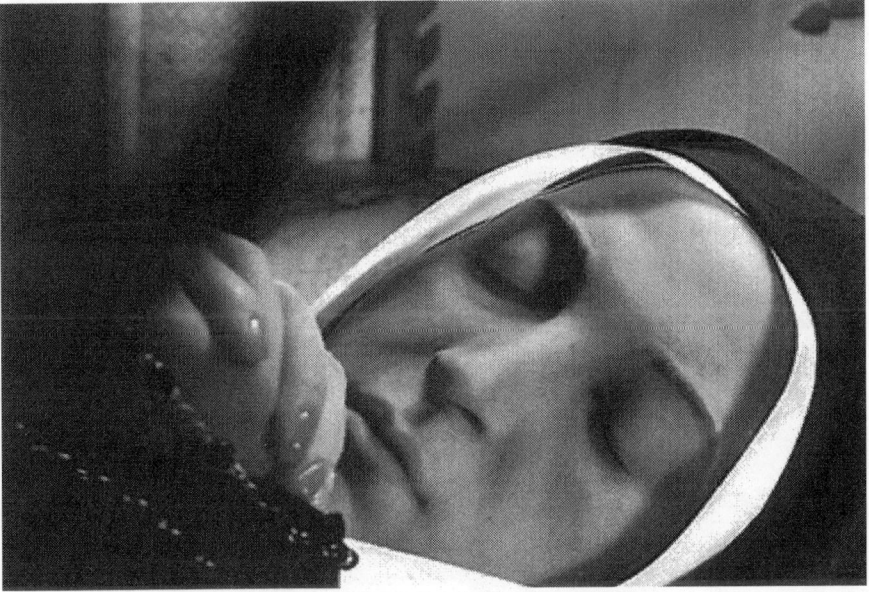

"Incorruptible" St. Bernadette.

The Basilica at Lourdes,

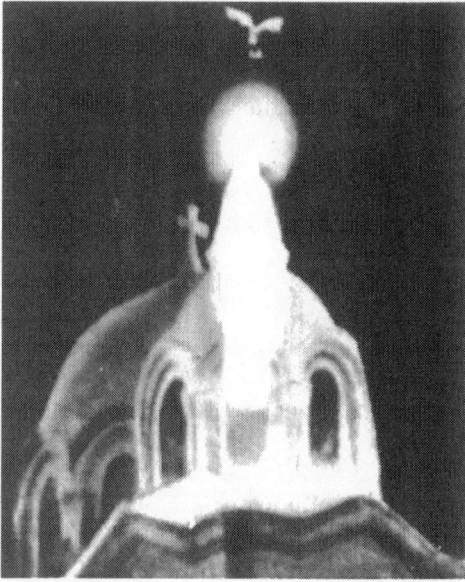

This photo was taken of the Virgin Mary with doves "gliding" around her.   Zeitoun, Egypt.

Photo was taken at Medjugorie by a pilgrim. The image of the Virgin Mary is <u>superimposed</u> on it!

**Auriesville, New York, and Our Lady of Martyr Shrine
I have personally experienced the "odor of sanctity" at
this location.**

**Mary instructed Catherine Labouré at
Rue De Bac: "Have a medal struck after
this model. All who wear it will receive
great graces; they should wear it around
the neck. Graces will abound for those
who wear it with confidence".**

Jacinta, Lucia and
Francisco at Fatima.

Statue of Mary at Our Lady
of Martyrs Shrine,
Auriesville, New York

October 13, 1917, crowd witnessing miracles at Fatima.

Weeping Statue of Mary at Akita, Japan

Chapter 9
Our Lady of Fatima

There are many apparitional sightings of the Virgin Mary. A few might be described as "great apparitions". Fatima, like Guadalupe, Lourdes, Betania and Zeitoun, falls into this category.

This level of esteem is noted because of the pivotal timing of the event, as well as the dramatic nature of the apparition. Also, the huge number of witnesses, seventy to one hundred thousand, makes Fatima a milestone event.

Portugal was a poor country in the early 1900's. The village of Fatima was a very small settlement, seventy five miles from Lisbon, the country's capital. Agriculture and sheep farming were the principle occupations in this isolated region.

The war in Europe was still raging in Europe in 1917. The battlefields were far from Portugal, though Portuguese were involved in the war. The United States had not yet decisively changed the character of the struggle. This rural part of Portugal seemed timeless in 1917, it's peasant population being mostly unaffected by the Great War.

There were changes in the attitudes of those who governed Portugal, however. Though always a heavily Catholic country, the central Portuguese government was now in control of atheistic socialists. This group was antagonistic to the church, and sought to blame the church for all manner of social ills. The socialists contended that the church reinforced the long term status quo of rich elite and peasantry.

It was against this background of war and atheism that the apparitions occurred. This apparitional event also involved great amounts of prophecy, including the controversial "third secret: of Fatima.

Like many other settings, Mary chose to reveal herself to young, simple, peasant children. In this case, the three seers were 10 year old Lucia and her two cousins, Jacinta and Francisco, ages 7 and 9. These children helped their family by being shepherds.

Every day they would lead their sheep to graze, herding them up in the afternoon. The cousins were close, and enjoyed each other's company.

The apparitions started on May 13, 1917. After attending church on this Sunday, the children resumed their taking the sheep to graze at a place called Cova Da Iria. This was an open field, around which were a small patch of trees.

The children saw a flash of lightening, and their attention was drawn to a small tree. A beautiful woman was described as hovering over this tree. This lady said she would appear to the children on the thirteenth of each month for seven straight months. Indicated she was from heaven, the visitor calmed the three children, and they were not afraid. Instead, all the children felt a powerful sense of joy. The vision ended this time with the lady rising up in the sky till she disappeared.

This initial visit was not dramatic, nor widely witnessed. The Virgin Mary did not yet identify herself, except to say she was from heaven.

The children could not keep these events secret. With adults hearing their accounts, the little shepherds were the object of ridicule. They were, of course, accused of making up stories.

Word spread throughout Portugal about the apparition, as more and more people were attending the events. A pattern was emerging where the first sign of the event was extreme lightening. Then, a white cloud would descend over the oak tree at Cova Da Iria. Only the three seers could hear her, and only Lucia could communicate with her. In spite of this, it was clear to other witnesses that they were witnessing metaphysical events.

Another aspect of these events also emerged, prophecy. It was at the second vision where the Virgin Mary told Lucia that she would live to an old age, while Francisco and Jacinta would die very young. Lucia lived into her nineties, and the other two cousins died within a couple of years. Other prophecies emerged concerning the world at large.

The third apparition, witnessed by 4,000, entailed a message from Mary that foretold:

1. An unnatural light would appear in the night sky
2. This light would signal the start of World War II
3. Russia, if not changed in its path, would wreak havoc in the world by way of its "errors".

Remember, these small children were hardly up to date on the world's political scene. The year 1917 was the year of the Russian Revolution, the rise of communism. To predict such an event would require knowledge that was clearly unavailable to rural, peasant children.

The prophecy that World War II would be preceded by unnatural lights in the night sky would come to pass. On January 24-25, 1938, Europe experienced what was described as an extreme display of the aurora borealis. This "northern lights" event was beyond the norm for this event.

Relatedly, it has been reported that Hitler was at his retreat at Berchtesgaden on that night. After gazing transfixed at the northern light display, he turned to his entourage and said the war could now begin.

This third apparition was also the beginning of the mention of the "third secret" of Fatima. After the apparition, Lucia was asked what was said. Instead of her usual openness, she said Mary's information was a "secret".

The seer Lucia, in 1927, told us the 3rd secret consisted of:

1. Visions of hell witnessed by the children.
2. Devotion to the Immaculate Heart of Mary
3. A third part relayed only to the Pope.

It was Mary's wish that the third secret not be revealed till 1960, at the earliest. Lucia told the first two parts of the prophecies to her confessors in 1927. This recorded the prophecy of World War II, and Russia's "errors".

Pope, after Pope, had refused to reveal the complete "third secret". Pope John Paul II finally consecrated Russia to the Immaculate Heart of Mary in 1984.

At the time of this writing, it is currently being debated whether Russian is now more Christian than the United States of America. Putin and Medvedev are constantly attending services at Russian Orthodox churches. The Russian federal government is spending hundreds of millions to refurbish deteriorated churches from the communist era. Is it possible these developments are the result of Pope John Paul's actions in 1984? Maybe this moderation of Russian attitudes precluded a nuclear war? I personally witnessed Vladimir Putin saying, much to the 60 Minutes' correspondents' chagrin, "God bless the American people".

As to the much discussed "third secret", it has been described as having to do with natural catastrophes. Could the tsunamis and earthquakes, of recent years, be what Mary was warning of?

This brings us to the culminating apparition at Fatima on October 13, 1917. Mary had promised the seers a true miracle on that day, and it happened.

Anticipation of this great day had been building for six months. The crowd at the fifth apparition in September numbered somewhere between twenty-five thousand and thirty thousand. This crowd absolutely dwarfed that figure. Estimates of the October crowd's size range between eighty and on hundred thousand. People were arriving from all corners of Portugal, as well as other European countries.

The faithful were, of course, interested in Mary's final visit. The skeptics, and enemies of the church, were looking for an opportunity to paint the church in a bad light. Newspapers were well represented at this event, making it one of the most evaluated events in world history, to that date.

The weather was abysmal. A light, but steady rain had been falling that made the Cova Da Iria a muddy quagmire. Thousands were waiting in discomfort to witness the Divine.

The Virgin Mary appeared to the three children, describing herself as, "Our Lady of the Rosary". At the end of the apparition, Mary began to rise up from her position in front of the children.

Lucia cried out as the sun broke through the clouds. The sun was not the usual blinding version of our sun, but one that could be viewed with the naked eye. It began spinning on its axis, changing colors from yellow to blue. The sung began to "dance" in the sky, and at one point, looked like it was going to strike the earth. The crowd was terrified, praying for mercy. The crowd, thoroughly soaked in the constant rain, was miraculously dry. All these events were recorded in great detail by many reporters, formerly antagonistic to the church. Funny, once one gets to be a witness to the paranormal all the "snickering" is silent. No one I've been able to uncover debunked this event. Many were convinced as a result of the experience.

Francisco and Jacinta, died within a few years, as Mary predicted. Lucia lived to a very old age, dying at age 97 in 2005, also as Mary predicted.

Given all the testimony of the witnesses, fulfilled prophecy, and remarkable physical events, one would have to classify Fatima as an astounding event.

Chapter 10
Two Belgian Apparitions

The little country of Belgium was host to two Vatican approved apparitions in the early 1930's. One occurred at Beauraing in 1932, and the other at Banneaux in 1933.

Belgium has had the misfortune to border France, the historic enemy of Germany. Two different times Belgium has been subject to enormous atrocities at the hands of the Germans, in spite of Belgian neutrality.

Beauraing was in the Ardennes region of World War I fame. It was another remote location, close to the French border.

There was a convent school, the sisters of Christian Doctrine that was attended by Gilberte Voisin. On November 29, 1932, her brother and sister went to pick Gilberte up from school. The two Degeimbro sisters also accompanied them to the school.

All of the children saw an unusual glow around a statue to Our Lady of Lourdes. This experience completely unsettled all five children. They had a similar experience on each of the next two days.

The third day all five children went to the school, and again saw the apparition. This time the Blessed Virgin Mary did acknowledge who she was. She said she would be back on the feast of the Immaculate Conception, December 8th. She also said she wanted a chapel to be built in her honor in Beauraing.

The entire country of Belgium was electrified with news of the apparitions. On December 8th, the Virgin was good to her word, and did make another appearance. Ten thousand were in attendance, from all points of the compass. Various doctors were present to test the seers, as they went into a religious "ecstasy" during the apparition. The seers, as in other cases, were oblivious to their surroundings, and pain. They were stabbed with needles, and even burned. They would not flinch, or even blink.

Various efforts were made to ask Mary to perform miracles as proof of her reality, but as of mid December they were ignored.

There were messages given individually to the seers, described as being somewhat dark and "gloomy".

It was not until June of 1933 that the miracles began to happen at Beauraing.

A 58 year old man, Tilman Come, made a pilgrimage to Beauraing out of desperation. He was suffering spondylitis, resulting in extreme joint stiffening. Come went into a series of painful spasms, and emerged from the care he was traveling in. He walked out of the car!

Come claimed to have had an interior vision of the Virgin Mary. He reported her saying, "I have come here for the glory of Belgium and to preserve this land from the invader. You must make haste". The notion implied is conversion of the heart, and prayer, would avert disaster.

At this time, remember that France had the largest land army in the world. Also, it was their job to be a "check" on the German's military ambitions. (This being a legacy from World War I). Hitler himself was named *Time Magazine* "Man of the Year" in 1935. All this made the idea of another invasion of Belgium seem very remote. These predictions were astounding in their accuracy, going against all that was considered possible at the time.

After Come's dramatic cure, pilgrims came in the millions to Beauraing. For a period of time, more came to Beauraing than Lourdes from pilgrimages.

On July 2nd, 1949, the local bishop affirmed that Mary really did appear to the seers of Beauraing. Cures continue to the present day.

Banneaux is approximately 50 miles north of Beauraing. A twelve year old girl, Mariette Beco, began seeing visions of the Virgin Mary, starting on January 15, 1933.

Mariette's family was upset at the notion that their daughter was a seer. The general consensus was that this was just an imitation of Beauraing. This was also the initial attitude of the local clergy.

Mariette described the Virgin appearing as she had in various other appearances. She had a bright white dress, high collar, and a blue sash of a brilliant shade. Mary appears this way in most, but not all appearances.

Mary did show Mariette a stream, saying: "This spring is set apart for me".
The spring was supposed to bring cures to the sick. Mary also described herself, saying, "I am the Blessed Virgin of the Poor".

Within another year, the spring's water was being bottled, and distributed worldwide. As a pilgrimage site, Banneaux began to be heavily frequented. Many investigators looked into the details, and found no evidence of fraud.

The Vatican itself approved the apparitions at both Beauraing and Banneaux. In both of these cases, no effort was made to profit financially from the apparitions by the seers. The prophecies from Beauraing and the cures from Banneaux, are very hard to either debunk or overlook!

I don't mean to trivialize what is holy, and obviously important to me. But, being an old Florida salesman, I'm reminded of a saying from my part of the country: "If it looks like a duck, and quacks like a duck, it's a duck!" A little girl comes up with unlikely, accurate prophecies of world events. Another one finds a "healing" spring with verifiable results. I'd say someone helped them. The same someone who has been visiting since 40 A.D.!

Chapter 11
Apparitions to Saints

This chapter deals with apparitions which are more a form of personal revelation, than the more dramatic public messages of the Virgin Mary. Indeed, if one could chronicle this personal revelation phenomenon it would probably number in the thousands. The seers in this case are all either priest or nuns. Actually, they have all been elevated to the level of sainthood. God has a personal relationship with His human creations.

Saint Margaret Mary Alacoque became a nun in 1672, at the Visitation Convent Paray-le-Monail, France. Margaret Mary was blessed to have an apparition of both Jesus and Mary. (As did Catherine Loubore'). Saint Margaret Mary recorded His words: "Behold this heart which has loved humans so much that it has spared nothing, even to exhausting and consuming itself, in order to testify to them it's love; and in return I receive from the greater number nothing but ingratitude by reason of their irreverence and sacrileges, and by the coldness and contempt which they show Me in this Sacrament of love. But what I feel the most keenly is that it is hears which are consecrated to Me, the treat Me thus".

In a mystical sense, Jesus placed His love of humanity into the heart of Saint Mary Margaret. He further said to her: "Behold, My beloved, a precious proof of My love. I enclose in your heart a little spark of the most ardent flame of My love to serve you as a heart, and to consume you until your last moment. Until now you have taken the name only of My servant. From now on you shall be called the well-beloved disciple of my heart...If My people return even a little portion of My love, I will consider as naught all I have done for them...They meet My love with coolness and rebuffs. Will you console and rejoice with Me by supplying as much as you are able for their ingratitude? Fear not for behold in My heart is all that is wanting in humanity. I am their strength".

Saint Margaret Mary was given the task of spreading this condensed message from Jesus, emphasizing the depth of His love for us.

This level of love, with its intensely personal relationship for His charges, is very comforting. Eucharistic adoration, and the Rosary prayers, also encourages a deeper, more devoted faith. Perhaps, this book could be considered an example of Catholic evangelism. With these messages, and devotionals, it would seem like Catholicism fosters the level of prayerful relationship that Christianity calls for.

The Virgin Mary also had a message for Mary Margaret, saying: "Come, my beloved daughters of the visitation, approach, for I wish to make you the depository of this precious treasure, the Sacred Heart of my son Jesus Christ. You sons of the Society of Jesus have a great part in this precious treasure; for it is given to the daughters of the Visitation to make it known and loved, and to distribute it to others. To the fathers of the Society is given the commission to make the value and utility of the Sacred Heart of Jesus, the fruitful source of graces and blessings shall produce fruits above you hopes and labors; and the same for the perfection and salvation of each one of our in particular".

This concept of a Sacred Heart of Jesus, though foreign to Protestants, is very compelling. It is the same Jesus for both, and His love for us should not be taken for granted. These apparitions also emphasize that He knows we often <u>do</u> take Him for granted.

St. Pio of Pietrecelina, also known as Padre Pio, was one of the most powerful spiritual figures of the twentieth century. A great many spiritual gifts were associated with Padre Pio: Prophecy, stigmata, bi-location, and apparitions of the Virgin Mary. He has even been called the "St. Francis for our times".

Pio was born on May 25, 1887, in Pietrecelina Italy. This is a small town in south-central Italy, non-descript, though with a rural charm. His parents were Grazio and Maria Forgione. They were essentially poor financially, yet possessing a powerful and devout faith.

From an early age, Pio was a spiritually sensitive youth. He attended church regularly, and had visions of both the good and horrific. He took his temporary vows of religious life on January 27, 1907. Not long after, in 1910, there was the beginning of a phenomenon that many devout Catholics have experienced the stigmata. This is the actual bodily manifestation of the wounds of Christ in both of his hands, side and feet. Pio was examined by doctors many times over the years, and the consensus was that the wounds were genuine. Actually, why would anyone fake them?

It has also been reported that during Padre Pio's life he experienced apparitions of Jesus, the Virgin Mary, his guardian angel, and St. Francis of Assisi.

In a letter to his superior relative to his guardian angel, Padre Pio wrote: "Saturday it seems the devil wants to finish me off with their blows and I did not know what saint to turn to. Then, I called on my guardian angel, who after making me wait a while was right there at last to help me, and with his angelic voice he sang hymns to the Divine Majesty. I complained to him for making me wait so long...To punish him, so to speak, for being late, I tended to avoid looking him in the face and to move away from him. But he, poor thing, came up to me almost in tears, so that I lifted up my eyes, looking him in the face. Then he told me, 'I am always near you dear friend, I always walk near you...This love I have for you will not end'..." The above reference to attacks by demons was an often repeated experience in Padre Pio's life. These attacks were frequently brutal in nature.

In September, 1916, Padre Pio moved to a monastery called San Giovanni Rotundo, for a period of fifty-two years.

As if all the above was not incredible enough, Padre Pio also was capable of communicating with people in a language foreign to him. This is called transverberation. If this seems too extreme for the reader to accept, remember the Apostle Paul demonstrated similar abilities in his sermons. It really seems our rational view of the world is way too limited!

The "odor of sanctity" is a very frequent phenomenon found in Catholic experience. (See conclusion). Padre Pio had a powerful fragrance that followed him everywhere he went. It was often referred to as "like a mixture of violets and roses". Note, this was not from wearing any form of cologne or perfume. It seems to be a by-product of holiness, pure and simple.

As to his feeling for the Virgin Mary, Padre Pio wrote, "This most tender Mother, in her great knowledge, mercy, and goodness has desired to punish me by pouring, into my heart so many graces that when I find myself in her presence, and that of Jesus, I am obliged to exclaim, 'Where am I?, Where am I? Who is near me?! I feel myself burning all over, but there is no fire. I feel close to Jesus and bound to Him by means of this Mother…"

This great priest was acknowledged to be a saint by Pope Paul VI before he died. Padre Pio died in 1968, and was canonized as a saint in 1999. His closeness to the divine was something we lesser mortals can only envy.

Helen Kowalska was born on August 2, 1905, in Glogowiec, Poland. She was one of ten children, born into a life of poverty. She was drawn to the religious life starting at the age of seven, when a strong internal call was felt.

After a period of secular employment, Helen started her efforts at finding a convent that would accept her. This effort was succeeded when she was accepted at The Sisters of Our Lady of Mercy at 3/9 Zytnia St, Warsaw Poland. The date was August 1, 1925. She was given the name of Sister Maria Faustina, as is the practice of religious orders.

On February 22, 1931, Sister Faustina has a vision of Jesus who told her to paint an image of what will become the Divine Mercy depiction. This is where Jesus is shown emitting what looks like rays of light from his torso. Actually, it is really a representation of the blood and water which came forth from his side.

This was the beginning of many different apparitions of Jesus to Sister Faustina. I recommend purchasing her diary titled, "Diary of Saint Maria Faustina Kowalska". Enclosed within it are the numerous messages from Jesus to her. They are powerful, loving, and show His concern for us individually. It outlines His desire to be merciful to us, to give us every possible chance to avoid a negative fate.

An example of His messages to Sister Faustina is, "I am more deeply wounded by the small imperfections of chosen souls than by those living in the world. These little imperfections are not all. I will reveal to you a secret of My heart: what I suffer from chosen souls. Ingratitude in return for so many graces is My heart's constant food on the part of (such) a chosen soul. Their heart is lukewarm, and My heart cannot bear it; these souls force Me to reject them. Others distrust My goodness and have no desire to experience that sweet intimacy".

"in their own hearts, but go in search of Me, off in the distance, and do not find Me. This distrust of My goodness hurts Me very much. If My death has not convinced you of My love, what will? Often a soul wounds Me mortally, and then no one can comfort Me. They use my graces to offend Me. There are souls who despise My graces as well as all the proofs of My love. They do not wish to hear My call, but proceed into the abyss of hell. The loss of these soul plunges Me into deadly sorrow. God through, I am, I cannot help such a soul because it scorns Me; having a free will, it can spurn Me or love Me. You, who are the dispenser of My mercy, tell all the world about My goodness, and thus you will comfort My heart. I will tell you most when you converse with Me in the depths of your heart. Here, no one can disturb My actions. Here, I rest as in a garden enclosed".

The depth of understanding of our personal natures, and the degree He is put off by ingratitude, is very impelling. As in other related Biblical passages, Jesus will obviously cast off those who are "lukewarm". Especially important is His desire to have a personal relationship with us, an internal one. Is this really any different from the evangelical minister's alter call? Maybe Catholicism and evangelical approaches are really not so different after all?

On October 6, 1938, Sister Faustina died in Cracow, in the beloved company of her fellow nuns. On September 20, 1967, Karol Cardinal Wojtyla closed the investigative process in all areas of Sister Faustina's experience. (This was of course the future Pope John Paul II). On January 31, 1968, the congregation for the Causes of Saints began their process for determining whether Sister Faustina should be granted Sainthood. Finally, on April 30, 2000, Pope John Paul II canonizes Sister Maria Faustina Kowalska as a saint.

What had already occurred on April 1993 was the adoption by the church of the first Sunday of Easter as Divine Mercy Sunday. The Divine Mercy Chaplet is a regular devotional of the church.

The apparitions to Sister Faustina, though personal in nature, are perhaps the most spiritual of all apparitional experiences. Zeitoun was the greatest of the public apparitions, but the Divine Mercy apparitions lead us closer to God, and His insights, than anything other than the Bible.

Jesus Himself instructed Saint Faustina, relative to The Divine Mercy Chaplet: "Encourage souls to say the chaplet which I have given you...Whoever will recite it will receive great mercy at the hour of death...when they say this chaplet in the presence of the dying, I will stand between My father and the dying person, no as the just judge but as the merciful savior...Priests will recommend it to sinners as their last hope of salvation. Even if there were a sinner most hardened, if he were to recite this chaplet only once, he would receive from My infinite mercy. I desire to grant unimaginable graces to those souls who trust in My mercy.

Through the chaplet you will obtain everything, if what you ask for is compatible with My will."

Chapter 12
Our Lady of Zeitoun

Surprisingly, most Roman Catholics know nothing of Zeitoun, the most dramatic Marian apparition. That is because the investigating authority was the Egyptian Coptic Church. This ancient church is a separate body, tracing its lineage all the way back to the evangelism of St. Mark. Roman authorities were on hand to observe.

Events started on April 2, 1968, and continued all the way till May 28, 1971. Some Moslem garage workers were at the city garage at shift change. They looked across the street at St. Mary's Coptic Church. On top of the dome there looked to be a woman, or nun. The thought initially was that it was someone wanting to commit suicide. The workers yelled for her to not jump. One named, Farouk Atna, pointed at the woman with his diseased finger. (It was due to be amputated the next day). It was healed perfectly the next day.

Another witness cried out that it was the Virgin Mary. That very same moment a group of what looked like luminous white doves started hovering around the lady. Within a few minutes, the lady, and doves, faded out.

The following week there was another apparition. After this second apparition, they started being repeated on a regular basis. They were always at night, the doves returning before the lady appeared. Like in other instances, the Virgin Mary was described as wearing a long white dress with a blue veil. A halo was seen forming around her head.

The entire country was mobilized with the nightly displays. Hundreds of thousands were present at one time to view the Virgin. Reporters came from all over to photograph and witness the events. Importantly, the lady was animated. She would acknowledge those praying to her with waves of her hand. This was 1968, and I doubt if there was anything like holographic projection equipment. Even in the remote chance there was, would the projection be animated and interactive? I would say, "Absolutely not".

The Egyptian government actually dispatched special forces troops to check door to door, for a square mile around the church. This was to check for any form of trickery. Nothing was found, period.

The background of the political situation should be considered. At the time of the 1968 apparition, Egyptian President Nasser was trying to unite the whole Arab world into a socialist republic. The Soviet Union was the backer of his ambitions, sending munitions and billions of dollars to Egypt. Remember also that Egypt was a predominantly Moslem country. While Moslems do venerate the Virgin Mary, she does not have the status as in the Catholic Church. In short, there was no motive for the Egyptian government to perpetrate a hoax.

Francis Johnston, in his book "When Millions Saw Mary", quotes Coptic Bishop Grogorius saying, "The events have no equal in the past, neither in the east nor in the west. St. Mary has appeared in many different forms since 2 April 1968...the most glorious apparitions occurred between 27 April and 15 May. Before the apparitions take place, some birds that look like pigeons (others described as "doves")...I don't know what they are – appear in different formations. Sometimes two appear on the dome just as if they came out of it. However, the dome is closed; the windows do not open. They might be seen flying eastward, then wheeling about and flying to the west, and while one watches them, they suddenly disappear. I remember particularly on 9 June, the birthday of Our Lady (Coptic Calendar), I was at Zeitoun when I saw two pigeons very white, very bright, luminous, radiating light...They became tiny flakes of cloud, and seemed to enter heaven. They do not flap their wings, the glide. In a flash they appeared, and disappeared in the same way. They do not fly away, but above and around the centre dome. They stay quite near and are close to the church when they vanish. Whatever formation they take, they keep. Sometimes as many as seven of them fly in formation of a cross. They appear and disappear in formation. They fly very swiftly. They are not light on one side only, but are completely lighted. One does not see feather at all − just something bright. They are radiating creatures, larger in size that a dove or pigeon. Sometimes, as one of them flies lower, it gets larger and larger.

I have myself seen not less than ten forms of the apparition. Once I saw an opening in the sky, like the opening in the sanctuary in the Coptic Church. St. Mary appeared in this opening. She appeared larger than natural size, young, beautiful, all in light. It was the color of the sky in Egypt. She wore something on her head like a veil. She looked down towards the cross on the main dome.

She looked like the Sorrowful Mother. She did not look happy. She stood for as much as two or three hours in the same spot…She moves about, enabling all to see her. She moves very slowly. At time she has the olive branch in her right hand. Sometimes she lifts both hands in blessing.

The most wonderful scene I experienced was one under the northeast dome, above the icon of Our Lady. It occurred on the feast of the flight of the Holy Family. (1 June 1968). About nine or nine-thirty at night, a light appeared in the centre of the opening beneath the small dome, then very slowly it moved out through the supporting archway and took the form of St. Mary. It lasted two or three minutes, and as usual the people shouted to her. She usually acknowledges their greeting with both hands, or with one if she should be holding the olive branch or the Christ Child. She looks somewhat happy and smiling, but somewhat sad, always kindly. She then returned to the dome, and the figure again became a round ball of light, and gradually faded into darkness.

After about ten minutes, the cycle started again…As she would appear under another of the domes, or over the entrance into the courtyard.

It was St. Mary, in complete form that I saw, head to foot, very bright, no bluish, yet not hurting the eyes. No features were visible, but the outline was that of a very beautiful figure. This scene I saw countless times.

There is also the phenomenon of the incense. The smoke of incense, very bright, comes out of the large dome in unbelievable quantities. The cloud goes up ten or twenty meters or more. It is dark red. It then takes the form of St. Mary, as stars appear and disappear over the church".

Another description by Bishop Athanasius was taken by Jerome Palmer in "Our Lady Returns to Egypt": "Suddenly there she was standing in full figure...there was movement of the body and clothing. Our Lady looked to the north; she waved her hand, she blessed the people. It was something really supernatural, very, very heavenly...".

Given the level of the witnesses, and their sheer numbers, one would think that the American network news would have covered the story. The New York Times, the German magazine Stern, and others did cover it. Arab television broadcast it to millions!

Still, the question is, "why no complete coverage?" As a life-long network tv news watcher, I know they struggle to fill air time. This blockbuster of a story should have been <u>impossible</u> to ignore!

After the Egyptian Army investigated for fraud, the stage was set for the Coptic Church to issue its analysis. The Coptic Pope, Kyrillos VI, said, "Since 2 April 1968, the apparition of the Blessed Virgin Mary has appeared several time on the Coptic Orthodox Church named after her, at Zeitoun, Cairo...It is no doubt a real appearance, confirmed by many Coptic members of the highest integrity and reliability. They saw the Blessed Virgin's apparition and gave me complete details..."

Pope Paul VI sent observers who actually witnessed the apparitions. Various other clergy, Protestant included, also verified the authenticity of the apparitions. Even President Nasser was a witness to the apparitions, and verified that they were genuine.

Perhaps, there was a degree of pivotal timing involved in the Virgin Mary's visitation. This occurred just as the 1967 war with Israel had ended. It is possible that this event, which completely captivated the minds of Egyptians, moderated some of the atmosphere of simmering religious resentment. Christians, Jews, and Moslems all witnessed the Virgin Mary's appearance.

The government gave its analysis of the appearances as well. The Egyptian Department of General Information and Complaints reported, "The official investigations have been carried out with the result that it has been considered an undeniable fact that the Blessed Virgin Mary has been appearing on the Coptic Orthodox Church at Zeitoun in a clear and bright luminous body, seen by all present in front of the church, whether Christian or Moslem".

Even without verbal communication, or messages, this was the most potent of all apparitions. With the duration of the events, and the millions of witnesses, this was definitely a majestic experience. Forty-two years later, perhaps it can now be appreciated.

Chapter 13
Four Orthodox Apparitions

Most people think all Marian apparitions occur in a Roman Catholic setting. They are almost right in this opinion, but there are some notable exceptions. The Coptic Church had the greatest of all Marian apparitions at Zeitoun, Egypt. The Orthodox churches, comprised of many independent bodies, have had some important encounters with the Virgin Mary.

The Russian Orthodox Church can trace its lineage back to approximately 800 A.D., when St. Cyril and St. Methodius brought Christianity to Russia.

The icon of Our Lady of Kazan, originally brought from Constantinople, has great religious and cultural, importance to the Russian people. It was reputed to have a powerful feeling of the presence of God, to those who gazed on it. Pilgrimages were made to pray before this icon by the thousands.

The year 1209 marked the destruction of the city of Kazan, and the monastery that housed the icon. This occurred when the Tartars seized that part of the country. The icon seemed lost for all time, but that was not to be the case.

A 10 year old girl, named Matrona, began having dreams about the icon. Her dreams included instructions from the Virgin Mary as to where to search for recovery of the icon, from the ruins of the monastery. Followings these directions, the icon was discovered in the ruins in short order.

This discovery caused a religious explosion in Russia, at the reclamation of this historic relic. Our Lady of Kazan became known as the protectress of Holy Mother Russia. It was even claimed that the defeat of Napoleon came with the aid of the Blessed Virgin.

The icon came to be stored at the shrine of Our Lady of Kazan, in Moscow. The cathedral was destroyed by the Bolsheviks in 1917, but legend has it that the icon was smuggled out for safekeeping. Rumors, originating from Russian Patriarch

Aleksey II, are that the original icon is being stored at Fatima to this day.

The Ukraine was the original country in its area to become Christianized, dating to about 1000 A.D. The Blessed Virgin had been consecrated "Queen of the Ukraine".

Another remote setting for an apparition was the Ukrainian town of Seredne.

On December 21, 1954 a young girl named Anna saw the Virgin Mary after mass. Mary was dressed in her traditional manner: White dress, with a blue sash. She also wore her crown of twelve stars.

Mary gave Anna a warning to convey to the people. She said this was the "Age of Satan", and that mankind had better "return to God for relief of suffering".

This apparition was also accompanied by celestial displays of light, similar to Fatima. These signs easily convinced the skeptical that this was a real supernatural event, also like Fatima. The Blessed Virgin also condemned the clergy for "apostasy", not faithfully preaching the sovereignty of Jesus.

These apparitions again occurred, in 1987. This time the site was Hrushniv, Ukraine, a legendary site of past apparitions. The latest apparition in the Ukraine occurred in 1988. In her message, Mary said the following: "My children, all of you, are dear to me and please my heart. I make no distinction of race or religion. You here in Ukraine have received the knowledge of the one, true, apostolic church. You have been shown the road to heaven. You must follow the path, even though it may be painful.

The eternal God is calling you. This is why I have been sent to you. You in the Ukraine were the first nation to be entrusted to me. Throughout your long persecution, you have not lost your faith, hope or love. I always pray for you my dear children, wherever you are".

A thought might be raised here about the ecumenical message of Mary. She states the same feeling about love without regard for religion (denomination), as she did at Fatima. Perhaps Christians of all denominations should take note of this sentiment and view it as another likely proof of the apparition's legitimacy. She definitely is not lobbying for Rome exclusively!

On November 22, 1982, a miracle occurred to Maria Al Akharas, an eighteen year old resident of Damascus, Syria. Her sister, Layla became ill, and Maria prayed over her sister. Maria's hands began to exude oil. Two other women who were witnesses collected the oil and applied it to the sister, Layla. The sister was immediately, and completely, healed.

A few days later a small icon of the Virgin Mary began emitting oil as well. This was actually in extremely large amounts. Maria heard the words from the Virgin "Do not be frightened. I am with you. Open the doors and do not deprive anyone from seeing me". All this activity brought intense scrutiny by the local clergy. The icon was examined and every possibility of fraud was eliminated. Remember also, there was no monetary gain being derived from these events. In total, over 100,000 people witnessed miraculous events connected with the oil and healing in this case.

Mary relayed this prayer for us, "God saves me. Jesus enlightens me. The Holy Spirit is my life. Therefore I fear nothing".

This Greek orthodox girl was a recipient of apparitions for at least 7 years. Finally, the Orthodox Church acknowledged their validity, as a result of the duration and great number of cures affected by the oil.

The final apparition in this chapter occurred in Slovakia in 1990. They lived in another mountainous region, near the town of Litmanova. The Virgin Mary has a preference of remote mountainous places, as well as shepherds.

Two girls, 13 year old Ivetka Koreakova and Katka Ceselkova wandered into a forest near their home. They became tired and stopped at a wood cutters shack to rest. An incredible storm arose that seemed ready to tear the little shack from its foundation. The girls got scared, and they began to pray. Suddenly, the little shack was filled with light. The Virgin Mary was there, accompanied by several angels. The apparition did not last long, and it frightened the girls. They knew they experienced something remarkable, but it still unnerved them.

The girls' behavior was altered by the experience, and they seemed distant to their parents. The father of Ivetka pressed here to tell him what was bothering her. She told him of her experience.

Both parents insisted that Ivetka return with them to the shack. Instead of the typical Hollywood scene where nothing was unusual about the building, there was. As soon as they entered the shack, the light dazed everyone there.

Mary said to Ivetka, "Dear children, I am the Immaculate Purity. God has sent me to your world, to your times, with messages never before in history. Please pray, my children".

An Immaculate Purity medal was struck by the church to commemorate this event. Ivetka was a Byzantine Catholic, not an Orthodox one. Byzantines are a small group of eastern Catholics, under the direction of Rome. These accounts are very similar to the traditional Roman Catholic ones. They show the same God is in over all charge, with the same compassion for his creations.

Chapter 14
Our Lady of Kibeho

The country of Rwanda has been the scene of tremendous violence and depravity. The majority Hutus had a great, long lasting feud with the minority Tutsis.

Both tribes had struggled for dominance over the other one. At the time of the apparitions, the Hutus had reversed the traditional control of the Tutsis tribe.

About forty miles from the capital city of Kigali, there exists the small town of Kibeho. "Exists" is the appropriate term because the area is desolate, and frequently drought stricken. The land around Kibeho has been stripped of anything useful, as a result of frequent onset of famine.

Kibeho High School, though government financed, was a Catholic school for girls. On November 28, 1981, the original seer, Alphonsine Mumureke, had an encounter with the Blessed Virgin Mary. The sixteen year old was doing her lunch room duty at the school. Alphonsine felt usual feelings of both contentment and detachment from her surroundings all day. She had the odd notion that she was being summoned, or directed, by outside forces.

It was like Alphonsine went into another dimension, as the lunch room faded from view. A voice addressed her as, "My child". Alphonsine asked the beautiful lady who she was. Mary's response was, "I am the Mother of the world...then know that I am here to console you. I want your friends and schoolmates to have your faith, for they do not have enough. Now watch as I return to heaven to be with my Son".

Alphonsine's description of Mary was that she was very beautiful. She had a long white dress, and a white veil covering her head. She was neither white nor black, but rather a more oriental sort of skin tone. Mary also floated above the floor, feet never touching the floor.

Though Alphonsine was always fairly stable girl, her classmates teased her mercilessly when she emerged from the apparition.

The very next day the Virgin Mary returned to her, saying: "My child, I love you. Never be afraid of me; in fact play with me! I love children who will play with me because it shows me their love and trust. Be as a little child with me, for I love to pet my children. No child should fear his or her own mother, and I am you mother. You should never be afraid of me; you should always love me as I love you".

Anathalie Mukamazimpaka was the second seer who had an encounter with Mary, on January 12, 1982. Anathalie was saying the Rosary, and also became mentally detached from her surroundings. She was transported to a scene with beautiful grass and flowers. A white, dazzling sphere approached Anathalie. The Virgin Mary spoke to her, saying: "My child, I am sad because I have sent a message and no one will listen to my words as I desire...My child, you must pray, for the world is in a horrible way; people have turned from God and the love of my Son. As long s you are on Earth, you have to contribute to the salvation of souls. If you work with me, I shall give you a mission to lead the lost back from darkness. Because the world is bad, my child you will suffer...No one goes to heaven without suffering, and as a child of Mary, you may never put down the cross you bear...I cannot promise you happiness in this world, but I can promise you eternal happiness in the next world".

You will notice the last promise was the same the Virgin May made to Bernadette, eternal happiness in the next world. This matches what Jesus said that "sufficient unto each day is the trouble therein". This is, whether we like it or not, a purgatorial kind of world. Our job is to run the best race we can, as the Apostle Paul indicated. The third seer was another 17 year old name Marie-Claire. Marie-Claire had been a strong detractor of the other two seers. She went to every length to be cruel, and to ridicule Alphonsine and Anathalie.

On March 1, 1982, Marie-Claire had her first experience with the supernatural. This time it was of a malevolent nature, with bad, demonic visions. The following day she had an experience with Mary, finding herself in the same pasture of perfect grass, like the other girls. Mary comforted Marie-Claire, and said the negative experiences would not be repeated.

The essence of this experience is that demonic forces are in continual contention with the divine. The demonic forces must have been playing with one of Mary's seers. Note, the church has even found some apparitions to be from demonic sources-this is the reason for a long investigative process.

One message was given to Marie-Claire that was truly miraculous, given the circumstances. That was the information that every student that went to Kibeho High School, for the next six years would graduate. Considering the dropout rate in America, a rural African school would never have 100% graduation rates. In spite of the small chances, this miraculous prediction was accurate!

Another powerful message, given to Marie-Claire, was that Mary cared for all her children-regardless of religious affiliation. This was a theme in other apparitions as well. One would expect Mary would exhort everyone to be a Catholic, but it wasn't her emphasis. Mary asked only for a "conversion" of the heart. She wanted all to confess their sins to God, and love Him.

The Virgin Mary also told Marie-Claire that she came to Rwanda to show God care for all of us, regardless of race or wealth. I am sure this also applies to her visits to all those other isolated, poverty stricken locations. Somehow, the Blessed Virgin Mary appearing to remote, poverty stricken people has more impact.

Along these lines, Mary asked the seers to begin the practice of saying the Rosary of the Seven Sorrows. This was a modification of the regular Rosary prayers. In her message, the Virgin said, "What I am asking you to do is repent. If you say the Rosary of Seven Sorrows and meditate on it well, you will find all the strength you need to repent of your sins and convert you heart. The world has become deaf and cannot hear the truth of the word...This is why I have come here. I have come to remind the world- and especially you here in Rwanda, where I can still find humble souls and people who are not attached to money or wealth- to hear my words with open hearts...".

The fourth seer, in the Rwanda experience, was a 15 year old boy named Segatahya. Jesus himself appeared to this young man. Jesus said, "I am Jesus Christ...when you tell them you come in My name, they many not trust or believe you. For you to prove to Me you are capable of being my messenger, go not to the people working in the fields nearby to instruct them all to purify their hearts because the day of His return is coming soon...they can prepare themselves".

The fifth seer was Vestine Salima, a 20 year old from a Muslim family. Jesus appeared to her saying, "You will preach to many people who will come from far and wide t hear your words. I am Jesus, the son of God".

Mary appeared to her in 1982, saying: "What you have seen, I have shown you; what you have heard has been said by me. It is time to leave your earthly things and the life you know. You must prepare for the mission I shall give you. My daughter, you are being sent on a mission of love. You will remind the world of my Son's great mercy...I will give them strength to open their hearts to Jesus!!...Give comfort to the troubled and care for the sick. Never refuse anyone who asks you for help...Live as God would have you live".

Vestine became quite a famous preacher in the area, attracting large crowds. Mary went on to tell her that she loves us more than an earthly mother does, and would always there to comfort us.

The sixth seer to receive an apparition was Agnes Kamagaju. She was twenty-one years old, and a devout Roman Catholic. Her first encounter with Mary occurred on August 4, 1982.

The Virgin Mary came to Agnes dressed in a long white dress, with her trademark blue veil. Mary told Agnes that God had sent her with a message. The Virgin pointed to a "crystal ship", floating in the stars. This was, it seems, an allusion to Heaven. Mary also pointed downward to a great pool of darkness, the destination for sinners. Mary said Jesus wanted Agnes to help influence people away from that darkness.

Jesus Himself also appeared to Agnes and gave her a message to relate. The essential message was that people should not be so caught up in sexual pleasures, and the pursuit of wealth. They should instead look to God and serve Him.

The seventh seer was Valentine Nyiramukiza. She was 17 years old when she had an apparition of Mary. This occurred on May 12, 1982. At the time, Valentine was at a church service. The initial message from the Virgin Mary was that she was "the mother of God". Mary went on to tell Valentine that people had to learn how to pray. Her primary instruction in this was, "You must begin you prayers by offering God all you conceal in your soul". Then, as in the Lord's Prayer, we should forgive all those who we have a grudge against. Mary said if we approach prayer to God honestly our needs will be met.

All of the seers had a differentiate message, whether the apparition was of Jesus or Mary. The experience was a demonstration of compassion and hope for the downtrodden.

There were, however apocalyptic visions given to Alphonsine. These included death, destruction, and a "river of blood". Unfortunately, these prophetic visions came true with the mass genocide that befalls Rwanda. In the following years, over one million died in the continued feud between the Hutus and the Tutsis. This was out of a population of just five million.

Like Fatima, there were displays in the sky that were truly miraculous. The sun was seen as breaking into two spheres of different colors, and re-combining. Also, the images of both Jesus and Mary were seen by thousands.

There were also many examples of miraculous cures, defying medical experience.

Finally, in 2001, the church gave its approval to the apparitions of the original three seers: Alphonsine, Anathalie and Marie-Claire. Bishop Misago declared, after lengthy investigations, that the apparitions were of "supernatural" origin.

Chapter 15
Our Lady of Betania

Maria Esperanza, a native of Venezuela, had always been deeply religious, and a devout Roman Catholic. She was born in 1928, in Barracancas. Later, she moved to Caracas, the capital city.

As early as 1954, Maria began having internal revelations from the Virgin Mary. She learned that later in life she would establish a religious retreat. Also, the Virgin told her that, as a sign, on a December 8th, she would see a blue butterfly. Twenty-two years later, all this came to pass. This long lasting apparitional event is second only to Zeitoun in number of witnesses. It is estimated as many as 250,000 people saw apparitions of the Virgin Mary at Betania. As apparitions go, this one definitely qualifies as a monumental event.

On March 25, 1976, Mary appeared to Maria for the first time. She appeared above a tree, in a "cloud of smoke". The Virgin was very beautiful, with brown eyes and a light brown complexion. Her physical appearance was like someone in their late teens. This age factor matches with all Marian visitations. Remember, the angels who have made appearance also were very youthful. This is very comforting for those of us who are getting "long in the tooth".

Mary said to her, "Little daughter, you are beholding me with my hands outstretched with graces and wrapped in the splendor of light to call all my children to conversion; this is the seed of glory that I offer as Virgin Mother and Mother, reconciler of people, because I come to reconcile them. Reconciliation is the inheritance of my Divine Son. Little daughter bring my message to all. I shall keep you here in my heart from the day onward".

The second apparition, in August 1976, Mary said, "When all people of the earth take up their crosses lovingly, then there will be no more pain, weeping, nor death because they will live rising each day with my most beloved Son".

At another apparition, December 8, 1977, the long prophesied blue butterflies were seen by Maria, and many of her friends. Included also was the scent of roses, and other flowers, which occurred without explanation. (See conclusion)

One of the sweetest messages given by Mary was on March 25, 1978, "Little daughter, this is not a dream; my presence among you is real. Obey and follow faithfully this Mother so that you may be happy for all eternity. Accept the arduous task of bringing my message of love and reconciliation to the people of all nations. You will suffer, but what joy and happiness it will be to see that you have been faithful to your Mother. I take you by the hand".

In addition to the actual visual apparitions of Mary and the odor of sanctity, there were many displays in the sky. They were, as in Fatima, with the sun seeming to split in two. A vision of all three members of the Holy Family was seen periodically.

The most famous of the phenomena in Betania was that of the Eucharist. Bishop Pio Bello Ricardo relates an event that happened on December 8, 1991. Fifteen thousand people were in attendance at mass. A brilliant rose colored light was seen over the communion host. Then as Father Otty, the Columbian priest celebration mass, broke the last-it bled! This blood remained on the host for three days before drying. Also, it remained outside the wafer, and was not absorbed into it. It has been examined by clinical laboratories, and has been shown to be actual human blood. This is real, tangible evidence of the Divine!

Some of the many messages of the Virgin Mary:

On reconciliation

"Little daughter, I am giving you a glimpse of heaven...Lourdes...Betania of Venezuela...there is a place for all, not only Catholics...It is for everyone. There is no distinction of classes, nationalities, religions. This land is for the gathering of all those that wish to enter there!

It is your mother who gives herself, as in Lourdes, Fatima, Pillar of Zaragosa, Guaware…as in many other places where I continue to give myself. But remember: Here will be the light of the east.

This place will be a place of belief, of prayer, of faith, love, charity…you experience me and contemplate me among bushes and trees of this little wood that I have chosen…It is for this that I invite you to come frequently to tell me what you feel, you preoccupations, your troubles, your complaints, in short, all the hope you have, the doubts or anxieties. I invite you especially to consecrate your hearts to me, so that I may renew them".

Strengthening the Prayerful

"He (God), in His infinite mercy, will strengthen the steps of those who rise up in a service of continual self-giving, of dialoging, of teaching an appreciation of human values of a people. My people seek the truth of a just and fair teaching with moral values that will consolidate people and nations…Action and work are the axis but without prayer works are ruined…I, my children, will remain faithful until the end, following in the footsteps of my divine Son".

The period of apparitional activity lasted from 1976 through 1984. As stated, literally thousands were witnesses to all the various supernatural phenomena, and visions of Mary herself! The following is the official church investigation summary from Bishop Pio Ricardo, himself a witness:

"This Marian Year which we are celebrating by happy initiative of our Blessed Father John Paul II is an appropriate time to issue the present Pastoral Instruction on the apparitions of our Blessed Virgin Mary in Finca Betania.

Pio Bello Ricardo

Bishop of Los Teques

Los Teques, November 21, 1987

PASTORAL INSTRUCTION ON THE
APPARITIONS OF THE BLESSED VIRGIN
IN THE LAND OF BETANIA

Betania is an agricultural area which is located twelve kilometer from Cua, the parish of Our Lady of the Rosary of this diocese of Los Teques, a district in the vicinity of the State of Miranda, on the border left of the highway that joins that town of Los Valles del Tuy with San Casimiro in the state of Aragua.

In this spot, near the old and modest house on the property, there rises a hill from which descends a stream. At the foot of the hill forms a little cascade. From this, luxuriant vegetation grows like a vegetable tunnel, which ascends along the course of the stream. There is where the apparitions have taken place.

The first apparition occurred March 25, 1976 (Feast of the Annunciation of the Lord). The only one to see Mary that day was Senora Maria Esperanza Medrano de Bianchini. Other people's relatives and friend's (some eighty), who accompanied her that day, perceived only luminous phenomena and gyrations or movements of the sun. The same person saw the apparition again several times at the same site during the year indicated and in the two years following.

Besides her there are very few people who have declared seeing the apparition during that period, although they have testified to having perceived other phenomena as already noted: mist covering the mountain, brilliant light that reddened it, a profusion of flowers (non-existing there) which covered it, singing from an invisible choir, a play of lights, movement of the sun, etc.

From the time the first apparition was seen, centered in Betania, there was a movement of piety and religious formation promoted and directed by Senora Bianchini. There, people are reunited, especially at the end of the week on Marian feast days, to offer prayers and to reflect.

114

The Bishop of the diocese at that time, Msgr. Juan Jose Bernal, permitted some liturgical celebrations there. He himself administered the sacraments, especially in favor of the peasants and the neighboring houses. At the time, no formal ecclesiastical investigation was made regarding the happenings.

This situation, restricted to a relatively small number of participants, changed in the year 1984.

On Sunday, March 25 1984, a group of approximately one hundred and fifty people met in Betania invited there for the celebration of a Mass at noon. Once the liturgy was celebrated in the old "trapiche" (some sort of building), those present dispersed throughout the house to take some refreshment and to rest.

Meanwhile, some youths and children were playing near the waterfall. Surprisingly, they saw the most Holy Virgin appearing over and behind it. It was very brief and afterward, they ran to relay the news to those who were together about one hundred and fifty meters away. They all hastened to the site of the apparition. There they were commenting on what had happened when the Virgin appeared again, being seen by all present. During that afternoon there occurred seven apparitions which lasted from five to ten minutes, except the last at nightfall, which lased approximately one-half hour.

Naturally, the news of these events was spread among relatives and friends of those present. This produced a flood of visitors to the place, especially at the end of the week. The apparitions continued taking place with noticeable chronology, although generally on Saturdays and Sundays, and on days of Marian celebration. They were especially numerous during the years 1984 and 1985, more spread out during the years 1986 and 1987.

I-1. Ecclesiastical Investigation

The same week beginning with Sunday the twenty-fifth of March in 1984, there came to the diocesan curia the first witnesses who, spontaneously, wished to present to me their oral testimony of what happened and to give a written declaration.

I received them and questioned them kindly and openly, although as is normal for one having theological and psychological training and a knowledge of the history of the Church, having a interior attitude of doubt and skepticism. Therefore, given the quality of information and the data they were relating, I judged that the subject should be investigated seriously. As a matter of fact, I organized the convocation of protagonists and witnesses, no simple task, given the fact that the great majority resided in scattered, diverse cities outside the jurisdiction of the diocese.

I decided to personally conduct the investigation. This permitted me to line up efficaciously my personal agenda with that of possible witnesses, something that would, with great difficulty, have been possible if I had committed this task to a commission, given the number and dispersion of those testifying and the prolongation of the phenomena.

This option, as is obvious, obliged me to dedicate very much time to this subject, some four hundred to five hundred hours; but it has permitted me to interview with calm, approximately two hundred protagonists, and to gather study and file three hundred and eighty-one written declarations. The majority of these were given during the course of the interviews. Considering that some of these testimonies were drawn up collectively, the number of people who confirm those declarations is four hundred and ninety. During this process, I abided by the criteria already classified in the Church, for the examination of this type of phenomena. I was preoccupied, above all, to determine the credibility of the witnesses; their background as people and as Christians, their sincerity, their mental state, their capacity for criteria, their critical sense, and their emotional equilibrium.

That credibility established, I tried to discern up to what point that might have been influenced by individual or collective suggestion.

I examined the spiritual effects or purely psychological effects produced in the people, such as the conduct of the groups that frequent the sight of the apparitions and especially the characteristics of the groups that, apart from them, have been forming themselves in a way of a movement of spirituality.

During my "ad limina" visit to Rome in September of 1984, I was received into the Scared Congregation for the Doctrine of Faith. I deposited there a provisional report on the events and I was given a document for private use, worked out for said Congregation in 1978, with norms about the process that has to be followed to judge presumed apparitions or revelations. With satisfaction, I verified that the investigation, which up to that moment had been made, conformed to the criteria and proceeding which are indicated in that document and which, since then, have constituted my work guide.

I-2. Characteristics of the Apparitions

a. Identification

In other apparitions of the most Holy Virgin, Her figure could be identified by how much was presented in the same form with the same features and dress, which gave rise afterwards to her representation by means of images or paintings.

In the present case, the apparitions have been presented in various forms, through which the observers according to the resemblance to know Marian titles, the most frequent descriptions being, "like the Virgin of Lourdes" (by the white dress and blue sash, although they show that the arms are extended, a sign of greeting or welcome, and that the veil permits the hair to be seen, or also "like the Miraculous Virgin" possibly by the position of the arms and by the rays of light that come from the hands).

Although these are most useful descriptions, there are also others, corresponding to the various Marian titles. The same concerned people have interpreted this circumstance as a teaching of the most Holy Virgin, who has wished t tell in detail that the titles are accessories with respect to her who is unique.

Already from the first apparition the most Holy Virgin presented Herself as "Reconciler of People", and this is the title or name by which she is recognized and venerated in this place.

b. Messages

There are very few people who claim to have held any verbal communication with the most Holy Virgin and to have received from her any instruction, message or counsel. Generally, they state in interrogations or in written testimonies that they have only seen and invoked her.

With regard to the content of the communications that bear witness to the ones that they have received during the apparitions, I point out the following factors:

-Renewal of faith, as especially urgent in a world in which so many deny God and cast off the supernatural, or practically dispense with God and the supernatural in their life.

-Deepening faith, through reading and reflection on the Word of God in Scared Scripture.

-Conversion from sin, and a full Christian life.

-Apostolic commitment is a consequence of that renewed, deepened and lively faith.

-A call to prayer, as communication with God, and finally for Church, for priests, for vocation, for the conversation of sinners, for peace in the world, for the imminent dangers that threaten humanity.

-Frequent reception of the sacraments, especially reconciliation and the Eucharist.

-Solidarity, called to charity, especially with those most in need, the poor, those living on the fringes of society, the sick; persistence in brotherly tolerance, and the sense of each one sharing what he has with the rest.

In other cases the apparitions have been seen by a privileged few. In this situation, the number of witnesses is numerous, from the 25th of March 1984. That specific day one hundred people say the seven apparitions: at least one hundred and eight gave testimony the same day with their signatures.

From that day witnesses were multiplying. With the exception of the day immediately before the one indicated, the norm has been that of a group of people present with only a few of them seeing the apparitions. Also it has been characteristic that those who on some occasion may have seen the apparition, on other occasions they have not had the privilege.

Leaving the oral or written testimonies received, and the data obtained, and bearing in mind that the witnesses are scattered throughout different cities, with difficulty to locate them and to make an appointment with them, I assume that, up to now, from five hundred to a thousand people have seen the apparition.

c. Quality of People

The usual thinking regarding apparitions of the most Holy Virgin is that those privileged, except very few, are of poor and uneducated conditions, and generally children or quite young people. In this case, there are at the same time, a number of economically well-situated people, of middle class, such as professional people of different university specialties; among them I mention medicine, psychiatry, psychology, engineering, and law. There are numerous students from different universities in Caracas.

d. Chronology

I pointed out before that the apparitions have not had an announced and predictable chronology or an established time period. Although generally they have taken place on Saturday, Sundays or on Marian liturgical feasts, they have also been taking place on unexpected week days.

e. Expectation

In relation to the foregoing characteristic, on numerous occasions, the hope seemed thwarted, for some of the people who had come to the place in the belief that some day on a Marian feast there would be apparitions, they, in fact, did not take place. On the other hand, on other occasions, a surprise apparition took place on

March 25, 1984 in which the intention was simply to be present at an outdoor Mass on the property and to spend a day of enjoyment along the edge of a beautiful river in the pleasant rustic atmosphere. There are numerous statements to his a given fact, that for the witnesses a totally unexpected and unforeseen surprise took place. The instances of those who have gone out of idle curiosity, skeptically or even mockingly, or to enjoy a picnic at the end of the week and have seen the apparition which has transformed them, are not few.

f. Sense of Reality

There is a classical example in other apparitions where the visionaries fall into a psychological state of mystical or ecstatic trance. Apart from this, I tried to determine during the course of the visions, and upon studying the written testimonies, whether in this case the loss of the sense of reality was present during the apparitions. I did not find such a phenomenon.

Of course, the visionaries are emotional but, with the exception of few who have suffered weakness as a consequence of the emotion, they maintain the sense of reality during the course of the apparition. They speak of and compare among themselves the characteristics of what they are seeing. They also intend to explain them to one another for natural reasons (reflexes, tricks, suggestions, etc.) to be convinced that such reasons do not explain the reality of their vision. At most, some say that they have felt absorbed in thought during the apparition.

This characteristic facilitated my investigation on being able to dispense with the technical examination about the purely supernatural or psychological character of the state of ecstasy reducing my inquest to the determination of the credibility of the questioning and the value of the testimony.

g. Concomitant Phenomena

Along with all the apparitions there continued to be present phenomena which I indicated on giving an account of the first three year: the mist which appeared to hover over the trees on the hill, the intense light that inflamed it, the profusion of flowers which covered it, the intense fragrance of the flowers especially the roses, invisible choirs, the perfume of roses coming from the water, the play of lights and movement about the sun, etc.

These phenomena have been presented before or after the apparitions and even without their having happened.

h. General Ambiance

I have verified that the gathering at Betania have taken place in an acceptable atmosphere from a religious point of view. There are serious occasions of long prayer, centered on the recitation of the rosary, the Way of the Cross and other current prayers, interspersed with sacred songs. The public is respectful and orderly except for the anticipated restlessness of the children. Cases have been presented of exaggerated emotionalism or hysterical reactions, but in general the atmosphere has been moderately balanced.

i. Effects

The effects have been good and some excellent, those who are present receive a strong injection of faith and spirituality. People, who never prayed, were praying the rosary. People, who do not go to church, no do so with regularity, go to confession and receive Communion. There have been notable conversions. It is consoling to hear confessions in this spot.

In all the interviews, I have noticed a disposition of receptivity for what the church officially decides. All recognizes having experienced an inner change in the feeling of drawing near to God and an impulse to a more Christian life.

I-3. Declaration and Judgment

From the beginning of my investigation, I noticed that it was not a case of fraud, collective suggestion or promotion of people or group interests by rather it dealt with a serious subject which had to be seriously investigated.

Relatively soon, along with my investigation, I became certain about the supernatural character of the phenomenon. I decided however to follow prudent practice and postpone all explicit statements about the phenomenon. With subsequent statements I would gauge the effects obtained and make critical pursuit of the religious movement produced by the events. I would then judge the opportune moment at hand for making public my judgment on these events.

Consequently, after having studied repeatedly the apparitions of the most Holy Virgin Mary in Betania, and having begged the Lord earnestly for spiritual discernment, I declare that in my judgment said apparitions are authentic and have a supernatural character.

I therefore approve, officially, that the site where the apparitions have occurred by considered as sacred, and that it be kept as a place for pilgrimages and as a place of prayer, reflection and worship in that liturgical acts may be performed, especially the celebration of the Mass and the administration of the sacraments of reconciliation and the Eucharist, always in accordance with the laws of the church and the norms of the diocese for pastoral unity.

I-4. Sense and Worth of this Statement

a. Competence

It is the responsibility of the diocesan Bishop to watch over and to intervene for judgment in every case of presumed apparitions or revelations that take place in the area of his diocese. The competence I derived from the hierarchical institution of the church and has been expressly declared by the Sacred Congregation for the Doctrine of the Faith on indicating the norms that must be observed re: said subject.

b. Sense

As I shall tell in detail in a later paragraph, this declaration does not have magisterial value that would hold the contents of faith of public revelation, which God has given to the Church, in Sacred Scripture and Apostolic Tradition.

Their contents are of divine faith and on being explained or declared by the magisterium are of ecclesiastical faith: who does not admit his sins against the faith on rebelling against God and against the Church.

In the present case, it is a question of a religious deed which is admitted for human faith, founded on the testimony of witnesses; given the circumstances in my own testimony this last as is obvious, especially authorized by the condition of pastoral guide that the Bishop has. The refusal to admit does not constitute, however, a sin against faith in that which every faithful member of the Church is obliged.

Who proceeds in such a manner will have to, nevertheless examine what his underlying motive is: whether it is prudence and a reasonable critical sense, or if it is a prejudiced attitude consequent to the scientific naturalistic mentality of those who do not admit except what is necessary for them with responsible evidence from mathematical calculations or laboratory experimentation. The skeptical attitude belongs to those who do not admit the possibility the God can communicate freely with his creatures and make invisible realities visible.

c. Pursuit

On making the present declaration I do not intend to affirm that all and each one of the apparitions occurring in Betania are authentic. I take for granted, as is customary to happen in similar circumstances, that her also there have been cases that are reduced to simple hallucination provoked by the expected, suggestion, emotionalism and finally psychological unbalance.

In fact, in my investigation of the case of Betania, I too encountered a few happenings that inclined me to interpret as fantasies and which I have refused as valid testimony. I have judged since then that the presence of these events, on the one hand predictable, did not take away the validity from the appreciable volume of numerous testimonies of those to which I concede credibility.

I-5. Public Revelations and Private Revelation

Faith is based on revelation. Throughout the years God wished to communicate with humanity by means of people privileged by Him for that purpose. In order that many truths thus taught by preserved,, He raised up writers who , moved by divine inspiration, wrote Sacred Scripture. This is, therefore, the fountain from which we may drink the water that gushed from the spring of revelation.

At the end of this process of salvation God our Father sent us His Son Jesus Christ, the Word made flesh. In Him is perfected and culminated divine revelation.

Jesus Christ, in turn, entrusted to the apostles, as His authorized witnesses, the propagation of the total content of revelation. Their testimony was gathered in the books that form the New Testament, and preserved also by contemporaries in what is termed "Apostolic Tradition".

The contents of Sacred Scripture and Apostolic Tradition contain God's revelation, and we must accept them in virtue of the faith which the same God deserves. This theology expresses that these contents are "of divine faith."

On the other hand, Jesus Christ, on founding the Church, entrusted to the apostles and to their successors, the bishops, the authorized magisterium. On doing so, He commended to them the preservation and authorized interpretation of the contents of the revelation.

When the magisterium of the Church intervenes in the area of revelation in order to interpret it, to specify it, or explain it, etc., given that by the institution of Jesus Christ and the virtue of the Holy Spirit it enjoys the charisma of magisterial authority. Its intervention must be accepted by every faithful Christian as content of faith, and its rejection is a sin against faith. The contents thus taught by magisterium, are known in theological terminology as "of Catholic" or "ecclesiastical" faith.

In Jesus Christ is culminated the divine revelation. With words of the Second Vatican Council: "He, with His presence and manifestation, with His words and works, signs and miracles, above all with His death and glorious resurrection, with the sending of the Spirit of truth, He brings the fullness of revelation and confirms it with divine testimony...nor is there need to await any other public revelation before the glorious manifestation of Jesus Christ Our Lord." (Dv.n.4)

And with regard to the interpretation of revelation the Council agrees: "The Tradition and Scripture constitutes the sacred deposit of the Word of God confided to the Church. The office of authentically interpreting the Word of God, oral or written has been entrusted uniquely to the Magisterium of the Church, which exercises it in the name of Jesus Christ." (Du n.10).

The previous explanation does not imply the affirmation that dating from the death of the last apostle communication with God ceased or that after Jesus Christ revelations are impossible.

It would be a contradiction of the history of the Church in which, if cases of pseudo visionaries and false revelations abound, there are also many visionaries, apparitions and revelations which unite conditions that theological criticism requires as a sign of authenticity.

Yes, it implies, on the other hand, an important difference. The revelation contained in Scared Scripture and Apostolic Tradition has, so to speak, an institutional character. Theology names it in such a sense "public" revelation. Whatever other revelation, although it may have as its end the spiritual welfare of the community, is designated "private" revelation.

What was properly entrusted by Jesus Christ to the Magisterium of the church was "public" revelation; and just as I indicated before when the Church intervenes re: it is obligatory for the faithful to obey and respect its decisions as "catholic" or "ecclesiastical" faith.

However, when the Church intervenes re: "private" revelations, it does so for the time being, to determine the arrangement of the same with "public" revelation. Consequently, if it finds that "private" revelation contradicts "public" revelation, it declares it false, since God cannot contradict Himself. If it finds agreement between the two, it allows "private" revelations to be accepted. Generally the Church does not exceed this planning, that is, it does not proceed to declare positively the supernatural character of "private" revelations.

Nevertheless, although it is less frequent, the Church can also declare that, having encountered sufficient motives which accredit the supernatural character of a "private" revelation, it admits it as such. But, on doing so, it does not oblige the faithful to accept this statement as "of catholic or ecclesiastic" faith, but rather directs so that they may prudently admit it as human faith on the guarantee of investigation carried out and the guarantee of proper testimony of the ecclesiastical authority that issues the declaration. Such is the case of the present document.

Aside from this, if anyone wished to study the apparitions of Betania to form his personal criticism, he may have recourse to the documentation referring to the same. For that purpose I have taken the precaution to make photocopies of all statements in order to preserve as untouchable, the original ones which I consider to have no substitutions for their historic value.

The apparitions and visions can be pointed out as a constant of the history of salvation. Through these God grants the visionary the visible perception of realities invisible in themselves, but not in the concrete circumstances of time and place.

Visions or apparitions usually include some kind of message or teaching, generally oral. That is why; it is accustomed to be termed "private" revelation; although also it can be given this type of revelation without vision or apparition. From thence, an authentic vision or apparitions, although it does not include any message, come to be an implicit revelation on showing visibly the existence of the supernatural dimension, and on exhibiting visibly, invisible realities.

To admit or not to admit the possibility of visions and apparitions depends on the position that is taken before the possibility that they exist and can be before the possibility that they exist and can be picked up realities which transcend the material filed of positive methods of investigation. Who denies the existence of such realities or the possibility of perceiving them, logically rejects the possibility of vision or apparitions and any type of revelation whatsoever.

Who believes in God, admits also that God can communicate with beings that he created. This possibility, of course, does not hold by itself that a concrete phenomenon constitutes a communication with God. It is necessary to purge critically each phenomenon in order to get the guarantee of what constitutes a supernatural deed. But the difficulty that exists to obtain that purification is not valid to reject, "a priori," its reality or to adopt an attitude systematically negative or skeptical

There are numerous visions and apparitions described in Sacred Scripture, as many in the Old as in the New Testament. With respect to the supernatural authenticity of the same, we have the utmost guarantee, that divine inspiration confers, for the content of the sacred books and those that the divine magisterium of the Church offer us.

Equally numerous are those that the history of the church marks out, now from its origins in the patristic period, up to our own times. They form part of the charismatic dimension of the Church which is linked with its ministerial dimension; although to tell the truth, the ministerial dimension is a charism.

As the second Vatican Council expresses it in its constitution "Lumen Gentium," n. 12: "The Holy Spirit not only sanctifies and directs the people of God through the sacraments and ministrations and adorns it with its virtues, but also it distributes graces, including special ones, among the faithful of whatever condition, dispensing its gifts to each one as it wishes (1 Cor. 12, 11) with that which makes them able and ready to exercise the divine works and duties that may be useful for the renewal and greater edification of the Church." And over the extraordinary gifts it observes: "The judgment of its authenticity and reasonable exercise pertinent to those who have authority in the Church, to those upon whom it is incumbent above all not to stifle the Spirit, but to test it all and to retain what is good." (1Ts. D, 12y, 19, 21).

This text gives us the incentive to understand the meaning that visions, and apparitions, and private revelations have in the life of the church. They pertain to its charismatic dimension; and they constitute a demonstration that Christ is present among us not the consummation of the world (Mt. 28, 20), and that the Holy Spirit, soul of the Church, acts in it and gives it life.

In some cases, to enlighten and guide a definite person; in others, to promote a specific style of spirituality or a distinct form of pastoral action; in others, to actualize or renew evangelical lines that routine had rendered inoperable or inconsequence had termed marginal; in other, for the solution of a crisis or the acceptance of an historical challenge, as Pius XII points out in his encyclical "Mystici Corporis": "Join to this that Christ looks always with particular affection at His Immaculate Spouse, exiled in this world; and when He sees her in danger, whether by Himself, or by means of angels, or That One that we invoke as Help of Christians, and by heavenly intercessors, frees her from the waves of the storm, and calming the sea, consoles her with that peace that overcomes all feeling."

In the scheme of thought we can interpret the providential meaning that the apparitions of the most Holy Virgin have, that, from 1830 in the rue de Bac, Paris, have constituted a series up to our own time. Typical of this century and a half has been the fact that man has believed in self-sufficiency, that his problems could be accomplished and solved by science, technology, social and political experimentation, human creativity, without recourse to God, and denying all intervention of transcended and supernatural factors in human life. Now then the most Holy Virgin who "advanced" in the pilgrimage of faith, faithfully maintained union with her son up to the cross (LG n. 56), and who proceeded the Church being the "type of the Church in order of faith, of charity and of perfect union with Christ," (LG n. 63) and "as Mother of Christ is united in a particular way to the Church that the Lord established as His Body" (Juan Pablo II, "Redemptoris Mater, n 6), and she does not cease to be Star of the Sea for all those who follow the faith." (ibid 6).

We may thus think that God has wished that Mary our Mother in faith, who kept faithfully the teaching of the divine mysteries (Le2, 19y, 21), and whose visit to Elizabeth constituted the first spread of Christ's mystery (le 1, 39-45), visit the church in these last times as evangelizer in a period of crisis of faith.

I-7. Reconciler of People

On appearing, the most Holy Virgin at Betania presented herself as "Reconciler of People." I point out in this paragraph hints in order to understand what this title means theologically.

The most Holy Virgin, her person, her prerogatives, her activity, her essentially Christ centeredness have meaning in Christ and for Christ.

Jesus Christ is our only Redeemer and Mediator, as Saint Paul categorically declares: "There is only one God, and also only one mediator between God and Men, Christ Jesus, a man also, who delivered Himself as a ransom for all." (1 Tm. 2, 5-6). Nevertheless, "the unique mediation of the Redeemer does not exclude, but rather stirs up in creatures, different kinds of cooperation shared from the unique fountain." (LG n. 62).

John Paul II applied this doctrine to the most Holy Virgin: "The teaching of Vatican Council II presents the truth on the mediation of Mary as participation in this unique fountain which is the mediation of Christ Himself." ("Redemptoris Mater, n.38).

As Mother of Christ Mary is mother of the church, which, is the Body of Christ. "Conceiving Christ, giving birth to Him, nourishing Him, presenting Him in the temple to the Father, suffering with her Son when He was dying on the cross, she cooperated in an entirely singular way in the work of the Savior by her obedience, faith, hope and ardent charity, with the intention of restoring supernatural life to souls." (LG n. 61).

The Virgin is, then, cooperator with Christ in His work of redemption. And that cooperation did not end at the foot of the cross, but rather "given by her Son as Mother to the growing Church – behold your Mother...her Motherhood remains in the Church as maternal mediation." ("Redemptoris Mater" n. 40). "This Motherhood of Mary in the economy of grace endures unceasingly...until the perpetual consummation of all the elect." (LG n. 62)

On the other hand, redemption can, also, be proposed as reconciliation of all men with God and men among themselves. Compactly Saint Paul expresses it writing to the Romans and to the Ephesians: "We were reconciled with God by the death of His Son." (Rm. 5, 10) "He is our peace, He that of two people made one, tearing down the wall that separated them, enmity...to create in Himself, of the two, one single new man...making peace...giving in Himself death to hostility." (Ef. 2, 14-16)

Being the most Holy Virgin cooperator in the redemption, she must be logically considered as cooperator in reconciliation.

In this role, she is the one who receives and proclaims the title of "Reconciler" or "Mother of Reconciliation".

That this condition of cooperator in reconciliation does not remain circumscribed in the earthly life of Jesus, but rather is prolonged in the history of the Church, we may consider it implied in the passage in which St. Luke narrated the event of Pentecost.

The outpouring of the Holy Spirit takes place as a consequence of having realized the reconciliation of men with God, and produces the reconciliation of men with one another, symbolized by the breakdown of the barrier which impeded comprehension with the multiplicity of languages. (hch. 2, 5-12)

In those circumstances the Virgin is mentioned singularly cooperating with her prayer.

The cooperation is prolonged indefinitely. "This motherhood (mediator) of Mary, in the economy of grace, lasts forever…until the perpetual consummation of all the elect." (LG n. 62).

If something has characterized humanity in this last century and a half it is guerilla warfare, violence, hatred among people and among social classes and nations, divisions of hearts and of deeds and wars. There have surged initiatives for peace and for union and there have been plans made for this purpose. But all the plans have been ineffective, because they have only touched the surface of human life. They do not go deep into hearts and souls where germinated as a result of original sin (the seed of hatred and division).

In the bosom of the Church has arisen the ecumenical movement which desires to restore the ecumenical movement which desires to restore the unity of all Christians in Christ. But this movement comes up against the walls raised during centuries of opposition.

And justly so. In this world and in this Church there appears the most Holy Virgin as Reconciler of People. She insists on the spirit of solidarity and mutual brotherly sharing. The title springs from theology on the cooperation of Mary in redemption-reconciliation, and the message holds much sense for the present day.

I-8. Conclusion

On concluding this Pastoral Instruction, I thank the Lord because He has granted to our diocese and to our country the privilege of the most Holy Virgin's visit. At this time in our Church history, symbolized by a new evangelization, it links us t the renewal and deepening of the faith and to the protection of that faith in a complete conversion in prayer and in apostolic commitment. In this divided world she must be presented as Reconciler of People.

The Lord wanted to grant us, by our Mother's visit, that outpouring of the Holy Spirit that He granted to Elizabeth when she visited her. And if on that occasion she proclaimed "from now on all generations will call me blessed, because the almighty has done marvels in me" (Lc. 1, 48-49), then through her intercession may be realized marvels in all the faithful who piously draw near to the place where she manifested her presence.

Given in Los Teques, Nov. 21, 1987 Pio Bello Ricardo Bishop of Los Teques.

I-9. Opinion of Mariologist Rene Laurentin

Rev. Father Rene Laurentin, Mariologist recognized worldwide as theologian and investigator, in his last work on the modern apparitions of the Virgin gives an account of those at Betania. After referring to the Pastoral Instructions of Monsignor Pio Bello Ricardo and citing the judgment issued about her, he says, "This official recognition is a new act, since no apparition had obtained any such authentication since up to the middle of the century. This explained because the Bishop, at once scientifically formed and endowed with discernment, could unite, without dissociation, the critical requirement and pastoral sense. As God's gardener, he has cultivated spiritual fruits from these apparitions. It has been for him and his people a fountain of well-being." (Rene Laurentin, Multiplication des apparitions de la Vierge aujourd 'hui, Editorial Fayard, Paris, 1988; page 54).

Chapter 16
Our Lady of Medjugorie

While Zeitoun could probably be considered the greatest of Marian apparitions, none can compare to the duration of the apparitions of Medjugorie. Both in sheer number and longevity, there is no parallel to them. The first apparition occurred in 1981, and the apparitions occur to the present day.

The country of Yugoslavia was a conglomeration of various religious, and ethnic, components. The primary religious were Roman Catholics, Eastern Orthodox, and smaller minority, Muslim. It has always been a seething cauldron of rivalries and discontent. Students of history will remember that the events starting World War I began in Serbia.

After the war, communism unified this varied collection of peoples. Marshall Tito, head of the Yugoslavian communist party, kept the union together by force of personality, and cruel oppression.

On June 24, 1981, two young girls had an apparition of the Virgin Mary. The location was the town of Medjugorie, part of the then province of Bosnia Hertzogovirda.
Ivanka Ivankovich, 15, and Mirjana Drageicevich, 16, were taking a walk in the early evening. They were walking on Mt. Podbrdo, near the town of Medjugorie. They saw the Blessed Virgin hovering about three feet above the ground. She was "shining", with a grey dress and white veil.

The two girls were, of course, in shock over what they saw. After returning to town, they returned with two other teenagers, Vicka Ivankovich and Ivan Drageicevich. The entire group saw the Virgin. Nothing was said to the children, at that time.

The following day the quartet of seers returned, along with 2 other children, Marija Pavlovich and Jakov Colo. Similar to other apparitional events, all six of the children could see the Virgin Mary).

The word spread quickly, and within two days a large crowd was witnessing the events. Also, as in other Marian apparitions, there were aerial displays of bright lights on the mountain. (Note: this phenomenon has been reported ever since).

The second apparition ended with the Virgin Mary saying: "Peace. Only peace. You must seek peace. There must be peace on earth! You must be reconciled with God and with each other! Peace! Only peace!"

The visit, and many subsequent ones, echoed this theme. These apparitions started a few years before the 1990's Bosnian War. The timing of Mary's visit was very similar to the circumstances of Kibeho. In both cases, the apparitions were warning to the populace, a few years before genocidal war. The difference, of course, is that Medjugorie has been ongoing for almost 30 years! Still, the pattern of prophetic warning is clearly established. In a very maternal way, Mary was doing her best to sway the Yugoslavian people from hatred and genocide.

The communist government at first dealt harshly with the young seers. Communism historically viewed religion as its natural enemy. This stance changed to a degree with all the international attention, developed by the apparitions. Also, with a flood of pilgrims, came a much needed cash infusion to the poverty stricken area.

A local priest, Father Jozo Zovko, was a champion and spiritual director of the young seers. The government imprisoned him for a year and a half for not curtailing the apparitions.

There have been three sites of apparitions at Medjugorie. The first was the hill called Mt. Podbrdo, also called the Hill of Apparitions. The second is Mt. Krizevac, and the third is St. James Church. The church is the continuing site where the Virgin Mary appears.

The picture in the front of the book has an interesting story to it. A member of my church, St. Elizabeth Ann Seton, Keller, Texas, gave it to me. It was taken by her companion, on one of their pilgrimages to Medjugorie. This photo of Mt. Podbrdo had the image of the Virgin Mary <u>superimposed</u> on it! Her features are both beautiful and clear. This is not any form of photo trickery. It is exactly what it seems to be – a miracle for the faithful. I feel it is my most prized possession. This phenomenon is hardly unique in the field of apparitions – (See the photos of Zeitoun).

There is an excellent devotional book called, <u>Medjugorie Day by Day,</u> by Richard Beyer. This is a compilation of 365 days worth of messages from Mary. One of the messages from 1988 was: "Dear children, again I call you to prayer and complete surrender to God. You know that I love you, and have come here out of love so that I could show you the way to peace and to the salvation for your souls. Do not let Satan corrupt you – obey me in this. Satan is very strong and therefore I ask you to devote your prayers to me, so that those who are under his influence may be saved.

Witness by your lives. Sacrifice your lives for the salvation of the world. Know that I am with you and am grateful to you; in heaven you will receive the Fathers reward, as He has promised.

And so, dear children, do not be afraid. If you pray, Satan cannot harm you in the least, for are God's children and He watches over you. Pray, and the Rosary always be in your hands as a sign to Satan that you belong to me".

Importantly, one should see, by the tone of the Virgin Mary's messages, that she is still a servant of God. She has been given an intercessory role that is an active one. Many Protestants see Mary as getting in the way of worshipping God, and honoring Jesus. How can this be when every message from Mary points to God, and her son Jesus? She is clearly <u>not</u> in business for herself.

Another one of Mary's messages concerned why she has been coming so long to Medjugorie: "Dear children, this is the reason for my presence among you for such a long time: to lead you to Jesus. I want to save you and, through you, to save the whole world.

Many people now live without faith; some don't even want to hear about Jesus, and yet they still want peace and fulfillment! Children, this is the reason I need your prayer. Prayer is the only way to save the human race".

Medjugorie has not yet been given church approval, but the Vatican is working on the matter. A commission is going to be established to deal with formal approval.

In 1989, Pope John Paul II was quoted as saying the Medjugorie was "the fulfillment and continuation of Fatima". Cardinal Schönberg of Vienna has thrown his support behind the authenticity of the Medjugorie apparitions. The cardinal characterized Medjugorie as something that could be "very important and profound".

Chapter 17
Pacific Apparitions

The Virgin Mary has been seen in all parts of the world, though no where as frequently as France. Many are not aware of authenticated apparitions in the Far East. This area is, for the most part, not a bastion of Christianity. Mary has appeared to Asians to show God loves them also.

There is a tradition in China that the Virgin Mary appeared in the village of Dong Lu, in the year 1900. This was a Christian enclave that was being attacked by thousands of government troops. The historical legend is that Mary appeared, along with the Archangel Michael, and scared away the government troops.

This is not the first time this has happened. Remember the German troops that did not advance, in 1871, at Pontmain France? Also, there is a historical legend that the Russian army was massed to invade Poland, in 1920. They were ready to cross the river, and capture Warsaw. The Russians saw an image of the Virgin Mary in the sky, and turned back. Hard to believe you say? Well, what did cause the Russian, German, and Chinese troops to quit their advance? Don't forget, all these events happened in relatively modern times.

There have been other, well reported, apparitions of Mary in China. In the same town of Dong Lu, thousands saw an apparition of Mary at an illegal mass, in 1995. One would imagine the Blessed Mother was honoring those saying mass, given the risks being taken in the communist country.

The Philippines, unlike China, is an almost universally Catholic country. It is estimated that between 85-90 percent of the population is Roman Catholic. On September 12, 1948, Mary appeared to a Carmelite nun, named Teresita Castillo. This occurred in the convent garden, located in Lipa City. The Virgin Mary asked Teresita to return each day, for fifteen straight days. She identified herself saying: "I am the Mediatrix of all Graces".

One of the miraculous events surrounding these apparitions was the spontaneous showers of rose petals. Some are in pristine shape after 60 years! This phenomenon has been attested to by hundreds of witnesses over the years.

Part of the final message to Teresita, in November 1948, was: "Pray. The people do not heed my words. There will be persecutions, unrest, and bloodshed in your country. The enemy of the church will try to destroy the faith which Jesus has established and died for. The church will suffer much...the love of My son will soften the hardest of hears. My motherly love will be their strength".

For many years, there was reluctance on the part of the Catholic hierarchy to authenticate this apparition. Then, in 1990, another apparition of Mary was seen in Lipa city. On January 24, 1991, another shower of rose petals again fell in the convent at Lipa City. With these new developments, the church officials did an about face in their evaluation of the apparition of Teresita. Ramon Arguelles, Archbishop of Lipa, approved devotions to Our Lady Mediatrix of All Grace, on September 12, 2005.

The above decision was also a result of apparitions which occurred in 1986. The Philippines were experiencing violent political unrest, just like Mary predicted in her last message to Teresita. Immediately before the resignation Of President Marcos, many were demonstrating in the streets. Army troops, in tanks, were preparing to devastate the political protestors. The Virgin Mary appeared, and that appearance caused the tanks to halt in their advance. Sound familiar? This was a well documented event, not that many years ago. Mary is there to reassure, and protect, like our own mother would.

Sister Agnes Sasagawa was a nun at the Convent of the Servants of the Eucharist, in Akita, Japan. Previous to joining the convent, Sister Agnes had a vision of the Virgin Mary. She was in a hospital where the Virgin Mary led her in prayers of the Rosary. Parts of the prayers were not yet translated into Japanese. In other words, Sister Agnes had unnatural knowledge which was well verified.

On June 12, 1973, Sister Agnes was in the process of Eucharistic adoration, when she experienced a powerful light. Accompanying this light was a powerful divine presence.

One week later, Agnes again had an apparition of the Blessed Virgin where they said the Rosary together. More appearances of Mary continued in July, 1973. Included in her experiences was the manifestation of her guardian angel. She was told that she would be cured of deafness. Sister Agnes had to function by lip reading.

Also, the statue of the Virgin Mary began bleeding. In addition to the bleeding statue, Sister Agnes received the stigmata, where she received the wounds of Christ in her hands.

The following is the message relayed to Sister Agnes by her guardian angel: "You have been suffering. Preserve carefully the memory of the statue of the Blessed Mother and engrave it on your memory. The bleeding statue is God's way of asking you for conversion, for peace; to make reparation for the ingratitude of humanity and for the outrageous committed in front of God. Pray for the conversion of sinners, while adoring the Sacred Heart of Jesus and His sacred blood".

Then, shortly after the message from the guardian angel, Sister Agnes heard from Mary, who said: "My daughter, do you love the Lord? If you love Him, please listen to what I say to you. Inform you superior of my request. In the world, many people afflict the Lord. I seek souls to console Him. To assuage the sorrow of the Eternal Father at His children's disobedience, which gives rise to His mighty justice, I , with my Son, await these who will expiate with their suffering and their spirit of renunciation for these sins of ingratitude. My Son and I unite with us generous souls as a gift to our Father. The Eternal Father is quite prepared to allow the world's people to experience the consequences of their spirit of disobedience and rebellion to His divine plan. I with my

Son have often intervened in the affairs of the world to mollify the natural justice of God which allow humanity to bear the consequences of their own choices. Our intervention has delayed the calamites that people have created for one another and for the planet. My Son offers all His suffering on the cross, along with mine, and all victim souls who unite their sufferings and penances to God as a gift of love. Prayer, penance, courageous sacrifice, mitigates the consequences or evil behavior…"

Several months later, on October 13, 1973, the final message from Mary was: "Listen carefully to what I say to you and inform your superior. If humanity does not repent and improve, the eternal Father will allow a terrible punishment to befall all humankind. This punishment will be worse than the flood or any that has been seen before. A fire will fall from the sky and annihilate large numbers. Neither priests nor will the faithful be spared. The survivors will be in such desolation that they will envy the dead. The only weapons that will remain will be the Rosary and the sign that the eternal Father will leave. Pray the Rosary every day. The devil's attack will be the most intense against those who have consecrated themselves to God. The loss of so many souls will deepen the grievous sorrow in my heart. If sins grow and become more accepted there will be no pardon for them".

A statue of the Virgin Mary began to weep real tears at the convent. This was witnessed 101 times by those present. The bishop and the congregation for the Doctrine of Faith, the Vatican, investigated all issues thoroughly. Samples of the tears were tested, and they were found to be real human tears. Included in all the occurrences, was the miraculous and total cure of Sister Agnes' deafness.

This apparition was found to be of supernatural character, and devotion to Our Lady of All Nations was allowed. It included prophecy, real physical evidence, and a miraculous cure. I would consider it one of the "great" apparitions of Mary.

Naju is a medium size city, at the southwest end of the Korean Peninsula. It really could be considered a satellite town of Seoul, only 20 miles distant.

Catholicism has a two hundred year history in Korea, brought from China. It was brutally suppressed in the 1800's because the ruling elite viewed it as a threat to Korean tradition. Pope John Paul II visited the country in 1989, and the Catholic population has swelled to the millions.

Julia Kim is the seer in this apparitional event, a local Naju housewife and beauty shop owner. She and Julio Kim, her husband, converted to Catholicism, after first being aligned with a Protestant church. Julia prayed with a friend who was sick, and he bought her a statue of the Virgin Mary when he was miraculously cured.

The statue began weeping tears, starting on June 30, 1985. It continued doing so from 1985 through February 11, 1992. There were a few months that the tears did not appear, but for the most part the phenomenon was a regular event.

Thousands of people came to view the statue, as word spread throughout Korea. In July of 1989, Archbishop Yong spoke of the weeping events saying, "The fact of tears in incontestable. So many people have witnessed it. We cannot prevent pilgrims from going there to pray before the statue. We cannot prevent the spreading of messages, of which a publication has been prepared by Father Raymond Spies. I am observing the facts, the development of events. I am examining the fruits…"

Julia's validity was also confirmed by Bishop Danchi, and the former Apostolic Nuncio (Papal Ambassador) Ivan Dias. This is a pretty powerful array of clerics who supported Julia's experience! Even Cardinal Sinn, based in Manila visited Julia, essentially endorsing her authenticity.

In addition to the weeping statue, Julia received 67 apparitions of both Jesus and Mary, during the seven year period. Most of the apparitions were of the Virgin Mary. The content of the messages was very similar to the "little way" of Saint Theresa of Lisieux. This was basically a call for us to be humble, and unassuming in our world view. Also, the stress is to believe, and trust, similar to that of a child.

An example of this sort of message from Mary is found in Julia's diary of June 14, 1987: "Do not brag about anything. Instead, have humility and love. Do not own luxuries. Daughter, let's live like a pilgrim and traveler-until you reach the bosom of your Heavenly Mother. Always be poor and little. Serve all in everything all the time. Daughter! While following the footsteps of the saints for the sake of Jesus, do not concern yourself too much with criticisms. Even when you get pains from others, give them peace. Through sacrifice and penance, do the things that can benefit them.

Everyday, lower yourself further thinking about Jesus on Mount Calvary. Through poverty, humility, obedience and purity, keep going down from the high place to the low place following this mother who wants you to walk the way of perfection. Shouldn't we become more humble like Jesus who chose to be humble? Change your life of conversion. Convert every moment, and converse with Jesus. Conversion does not just mean repenting sins. It means trying to lead a life that God wants you to live. Abandon the worldly life and live a life based on the Gospels. Live like a lily...Lets die again and imitate Christ".

Julia also, like Padre Pio, had stigmata wounds in the five places Jesus was injured. These were witnessed by many, especially Father Raymond Spies, her spiritual director. This spiritual sign occurs as the seer becomes close to Jesus. Also, in a very mystical way, the seer suffers for the sinners in a similar way as Jesus did. Of course, it is a miracle that underscored the validity of the seer and the message. Still, there is a sort of co-suffering with Jesus for reparation of sins of mankind.

One June 5, 1988, Jesus said to Julia, "I am still bleeding on the cross to save the whole human race and My blood will not flow in vain. I am the transfuser who washes away your dirty sins. My precious blood is a special medicine that will open the eyes of the sick souls-through priests. I am so troubled that people receive Me out of habit and with indifference. I wish to pour down all My love upon all the souls on this earth. Help them participate in the heavenly banquet (Blessed Sacrament). My mother Mary has often encouraged frequent confessions but many children make the confession without a sincere repentance or even try to receive Me without going to confession. A confession out of habit or without true repentance is an insult to Me, and will not enable one to see Me. Therefore, let Me work within you by confessing your sins with a sincere repentance…Come now, all the children of the world! Today, as always, I become a sacrificial offering and I am waiting for you…"

In addition to all the excellent aspects of this apparition, there have been many miraculous physical cures. Visiting the chapel at Naju, Julia herself was brought back from the brink of death by prayer.

One message from the Virgin Mary to Julia demonstrated a life of "lip service" is not what we need, "Did you see daughter! It is easy to start climbing stairs, but it is so difficult to complete all the fourteen steps (fourteen Stations of the Cross). Therefore, tell everyone to be careful not to fall of the stairs and turn all the accumulated good works into nothing. Good-bye".

Conclusion

God knows that we've become too preoccupied with our lives, and many concerns, to see further truths and realities. Jesus said "sufficient unto each day is the trouble therein". He knows we are "heavy laden" with life's burdens.

Also, in a related way, we have become jaded as a society. In times past, we tend to be more optimistic about ourselves, our government and leaders. A lot of naïveté was involved. Americans are usually more forgiving in their opinions than their leaders deserve.

The late 1900's were not good times for Americans, or the rest of the world. Our local (American) scene has been marked by wars, recessions and political scandals. Everything from the JFK assassination through the Iraq war has taken its toll on our world view. In the west, we have reacted intellectually to the past 50 years of strife and disillusionment. Traditional values and institutions have been rejected, in favor of a form of lukewarm humanism.

Scientific progress has also altered our view. The pace of change in our lives, caused by technological changes, has combined with the political disillusionment to make us less accepting of lasting values. Human arrogance has been enhanced as a result. We're beginning to think we don't need God.

The ironic part of all this rampant agnosticism is we are absolutely obsessed with ghosts. I even heard the "father" of near-death experience research say he doesn't believe in God! He said this profound statement after indicating his assurance of the reality of life after death.

God must be truly great and loving in the face of all this to actually love us. We are an arrogant bunch of misfits who reject Him, as well as almost every traditional value and moral.

God knows our predicament. He knows we need to be shocked out of our world view. He has followed the same approach since Biblical times: Confront mankind with holy manifestations and miracles. Faced with this majesty, our narrow world view vanishes.

The O.T. had God's real presence in the Ark of the Covenant and Moses' burning bush. Angels actually came to Lot physically. The Israelites were fed by way of a miracle with "manna" from Heaven. Moses actually parted the Red Sea with God's intervention.

All of the above were demonstrations of God's power and participation in human events. They also served as faith building proofs to the skeptical.

The miracles in the New Testament were even more extreme. Among them were:

1. Jesus turned water into wine.
2. He, and the disciples, healed the blind and infirm.
3. He withered a fig tree.
4. He foretold the future (Peters denial)
5. He raised Lazarus from the dead.

Also, the New Testament has angels visiting Mary, as well as relaying news of His resurrection. There is no telling how many of these truly miraculous events occurred which were not recorded.

Some of the most well documented and scientifically authenticated events are Marian apparitions. The tulma, cactus husk garment of Juan Diego, is an existing and tested artifact. Sandia Labs has verified that there is no tracing or evidence of pigment present. This fragile garment can be seen any day at the Basilica of Guadalupe in Mexico City.

The well documented events at Zeitoun Egypt in the late 1960"s rival any event for coverage and number of credible witnesses. Those that have an anti-Catholic bias should remember that these events occurred at a Coptic (Egyptian Christian) church.

The Catholic Church just approved the tenth apparition (Laus, France) in May 2008. Considering that these events occurred in the 1600's, one could not exactly say the Roman church rushes to judgment in these matters. The more modern ones like Fatima, Akita and Zeitoun were approved more quickly because of the incredible availability of evidence. These events are just true, period.

But wait, there's more!; A lot more! There is a whole field of study within the Roman Catholic Church in the area of saintly relics. Joan Carroll Cruz wrote an excellent book "Incorruptibles", covering this topic. As mentioned earlier, the bodies of certain saints have resisted decay for hundreds of years. Saint Bernadette, though touched up with wax to cover discoloration, has not been embalmed. Yet, her body has resisted decay for over 130 years.

There are over 102 bodies that qualify as "incorruptible". Besides Saint Bernadette, other notable saints that fit this category include: Saint Cecilia, Saint Agatha, Saint Rita of Cascia, Saint Vincent de Paul, Saint Catherine Labouré, among others.

To show the diversity in this topic of "relics", even the voice of a departed near-saint was included in Joan Cruz' book titled "Relics". This is the voice of Blessed Clelia Barbieri. (Note: The term "Blessed" is the category for an individual before the full canonization as a "Saint".)

Blessed Clelia's voice has been heard in the houses of her order since 1871, a year after her death. The voice is described as very sweet and audible, usually accompanying hymns in the Chapel. Her original companions, superiors and priests have sworn to the authenticity of this phenomenon.

The testimony of these witnesses has been meticulously kept. Tribunals have investigated this matter in detail. This lead to the church beautifying Clelia in October of 1968. The voice continues to be heard till the present day.

This is a case of a phenomenon lasting over 100 years, witnessed by credible, devout and religious people. Similar to the Marian apparitions, the degree and scope of investigation make legal investigations of the present day pale in comparison.

I have an ex-wife who is a devout Baptist. Sue lives in Springfield, Missouri. She was having trouble paying for the house she purchased in a nice area of Springfield. As with many people in our economy, some of Sue's investments had gone "south"! Sue, being in danger of losing the house, resorted to constant prayer in dealing with these anxieties. She was rewarded with a strong, and audible, message to get busy trying to sell the house. An actual date the house would sell was given her, May 15, 2008. Sue told her close friend in the church about the message. It happened just that day! I believe that this is another example that God is active in our prayers and life.

Finally, there is Auriesville, New York, and Our Lady of Martyr's Shrine. This beautiful shrine is located in the Mohawk Valley, 40 miles west of Albany on the New York State Thruway (Hwy 90)

In September of 2008, I flew up to upstate New York with the idea of buying property. I took a "red-eye" flight to Albany that arrived from Dallas at 1am on Tuesday. After investigating the property, I played tourist for a little bit. I went to the Cooperstown baseball museum, and then drove back towards Albany. I stopped in Fultonville on Tuesday night, planning to explore the Mohawk Valley on Wednesday.

I hadn't started my Mohawk Valley tour more than 15 minutes before I came across Our Lady of Martyrs Shrine. This exceptionally beautiful setting is comprised of approximately 30 acres, on a sort of plateau. Located on the grounds are several buildings, including a visitor's center, 2 chapels, and a museum. I would strongly recommend that one should visit the shrine's website and take their virtual tour.

The shrine is run by the Catholic Church, specifically the Jesuits. It commemorates the martyrdom of three Jesuits who were killed by the Mohawk Indians in 1642. This is also the site in North America where the first Rosary was said.

I was on the grounds, viewing historical plaques. Within 20 minutes I started experiencing an overpowering smell of flowers. Having strong allergies, my sense of smell is not very acute. This aroma was so potent that it flooded the senses.

I stopped in the museum and spoke with the curator. I asked what was so fragrant, as I sold trees for a living, and all I saw were pines and maples. The curator looked at me in a shocked manner. She said she had worked there for twelve years. There was nothing fragrant on the grounds, only a handful of flowers-20 acres away! Further, she said every now and then someone smells a powerful smell of roses. I thanked her, and walked from the museum towards the grotto where the actual martyrdom occurred. The smell of flowers returned briefly, for perhaps another 10 minutes.

This same experience was also present at the apparitional site at Laus, France. Also, I have personally spoken with several Catholics who have experienced this "odor of sanctity" at important times in their lives. These are not delusional experiences, but real and powerful manifestations of the holy.

God has reached out to us by the grand and powerful means of Marian apparitions. Thousands of witnesses have seen them. Physical evidence even corroborates their supernatural nature. He also, being a personal and loving God, manifests to individuals like in Auriesville. I feel people should know how blessed we have been. Thankfully, we're not alone. We are, most importantly, loved.

"Love our Lady. And she will obtain abundant grace to help you conquer in your daily struggle. When you see the storm coming, if you seek safety in that firm refuge that is Mary, there will be no danger of your wavering or going down."
-St. Jose Maria Escriva

Hail Mary

Hail Mary, full of grace! The Lord is with thee; blessed art thou among women, and blessed is the fruit of thy womb, Jesus. Holy Mary, Mother of God, pray for us sinners now and at the hour of our death, Amen.

About the Author

Kevin Cook has a B.A. from Upper Iowa University, and a masters in theology from a Protestant seminary. He is a graduate student at the Franciscan University, Steubenville, Ohio. He can be reached at kevincook22@hotmail.com or www.marianapparitionsarereal.com

Bibliography

Websites and Institutions

1.   International Marian Research Institute
2.   www.marypage.com
3.   Http:/campus.udaytow.edu/mary
4.   spiritdaily.com
5.   The Miracle Hunter
6.   Knock Shrine
7.   http://enwikipeida.org/wiki/zeitounapparitions
8.   Catholic News Service

Books

1.   Albright, Judith, *Our Lady at Garabanial,* Goleta, California, Queenship   Publications, 1992.

2.   Allergir, Renzo & Roberto, Fatima, *The Story Behind the Miracles,* Cincinnati,   Ohio,   St.   Anthony Messenger Press, 2001.

3.   Bauer, Judith, *The Essential Mary Handbook,* Missourit, Liguori Press, 1999.

4.   Badde, Paul, *Maria of Guadalupe*, San Francisco, California, Ingnatus Press,   1999.

5.   Cruz, Joan, *The Incorruptibles*, Rockford, Illinois, Tan Books, 1977.

6.   Deery, Joseph, *Our Lady of Lourdes*, Westminster, Mid, Newman Press, 1958.

7. Doucette, Melvin, *Our Lady of Prince Edward Island*, Prince Edward Island, 2004.

8. Franciscan Friars of the Immaculate, Padre Pio, *The Wonder Worker,* New Bedford, Massachusetts, 1999.

9. Garvey, Mark, *Searching For Mary,* New York, New York, Penguin Group, 1999.

10. Ilibagiza, Immaculee, *Our Lady of Kibeho*, New York, New York, Hay House, 2008.

11. Johnston, Francis, *When Millions Saw Mary*, Devon, UK, Maslands, LTD, 1980.

12. Kennedy, John S., *Light on the Mountain,* New York, New York, McMullen Books, 1953.

13. Kim, Julia, *The Miracle in Naju, Korea, Heaven Speaks to the World*, Gresham, Oregon, Mary's Touch by Mail, 1992.

14. Kowalska, Sister Maria Faustina, *Divine Mercy in My Soul,* Marian Press, 2008.

15. La Doucer, E., *The Children of La Salette,* New York, New York, Vantage Press, 1965.

16. Scaperlanda, Maria Ruiz, *The Seekers Guide to Mary,* Chicago, Illinois, Loyola Press, 2002.

17.   Sims, Sister Margaret Catherine, *Apparitions in Betania*, Framingham, Massachusetts, Medjugorie Messengers, 1992.

18.   Smith, Rev. William, *The Mystery of Knock*, New York, New York, Paulist Press, 1954.

19.   Sullivan, T.S., *Our Lady of Hope*, St. Meinard, Indiana, Grail Publications, 1955.

20.   Swawn, Ingo, *The Great Apparitions of Mary,* New York, New York, The Crossroads Publishing Co., 1996.

21.   Waters, Alma Power, *St. Catherine Laboure and the Miraculous Medal,* San Francisco, California, Ignatius Press, 1962.

22.   Weible, Wayne, *Medjugorie, The Message, Orleans,* Massachusetts, Paraclete Press, 1989.

23.   Zaki, Pearl, *Our Lord's Mother Visits Egypt In 1968 and 1969*, Patriarch of the See of St. Mark.

Appendix-Marian Research Institute Chart

The Marian Library/International Marian Research Institute, Dayton, Ohio.
Created by J. C. Tierney

Year	Place	# People Involved	Approval of Faith Expression (Prayer, devotion) at site.	Approval of Supernatural character
1900	Tung Lu (China)	many people	Yes	No decision
1900	Lucca (Italy)	several people		N.A.
1900	Tanganika (Africa)	2 women		No decision
1900	Peking (China)	Crowd		No decision.
1904	Zdunska-Wola (Poland)	Teen-age boy		No decision
1906	Quito (Ecuador)	students & professors		No decision
1909	Bordeaux (France)	1 woman		No decision
1911	Bruxelles (Belgium)	1 man		No decision
1914	Hrushiv (Ukraine)	22 people		No decision
1917	Barral (Portugal)	1 child		No decision
1917	Fatima (Portugal)	3 children		Yes
1917	Bat. de la	soldiers		No decision

	Marne (France)			
1918	Muzillac (France)	3 children		No decision
1920	Catane (Italy)	1 religious		No decision
1926	Marlemont (France)	1 child		No decision
1925	Tuy (Spain)	1 religious		No decision
1928	Ferdrupt (France)	2 children		No decision
1929	Pontevedra (Spain)	1 religious		No decision
1930	Campinas (Brazil)	1 religious		No decision
1931	Stenbergen (Holland)	1 woman		No decision
1931	Ezquioga (Spain)	2 children/crowd		Negative decision
1931	Izurdiaga (Spain)	2 young women		Negative decision
1931	Zumarraga (Spain)	N.A.		No decision
1931	Ormaiztegui (Spain)	N.A.		No decision
1931	Albiztur (Spain)	N.A.		No decision
1931	Bacaicoa (Spain)	N.A.		No decision
1931	Iraneta (Spain)	N.A.		No decision
1932	Beauraing (Belgium)	5 people		**Yes**
1932	Marmagen (Germany)	N.A.		No decision

1932	Metz (France)	N. A.		No decision
1933	Banneux (Belgium)	Teen-age girl		**Yes**
1933	Beauraing (Belgium)	1 man		No decision
1933	Crollon (France)	3 children		No decision
1933	Onkerzele (Belgium)	1 woman		Negative decision
1933	Harcy (France)	1 man		No decision
1933	Houlteau-Chaineux (Belgium)	1 man & 2 children		No decision
1933	Lokeren-Naastveld (Belgium)	2 people		Negative decision
1933	Etikhove (Belgium)	1 man		Negative decision
1933	Herzele (Belgium)	Crowd		Negative decision
1933	Olsene (Belgium)	1 man		Negative decision
1933	Berchem-Anvers (Belgium)	N.A.		Negative decision
1933	Foy Notre-Dame (Belgium)	N.A.		No decision
1933	Melin (Belgium)	N.A.		No decision
1933	Tubize (Belgium)	N.A.		Negative decision
1933	Verviers (Belgium)	N.A.		Negative decision

1933	Wilrijk (Belgium)	N.A.		Negative decision
1933	Wielsbeke (Belgium)	1 woman		No decision
1934	Roggliswil (Switzerland)	1 man		No decision
1934	Lucerne (Switzerland)	1 woman		No decision
1934	Marpingen (Germany)	N.A.		<u>Negative decision</u>
1935	Rome (Italy)	1 woman		No decision
1935	Valmontana (Italy)	Teen-age girl		No decision
1936	*Bouxieres-aux-Dames* (France)	2 women		Negative decision
1936	*Ham-sur-Sambre* (Belgium)	2 women		Negative decision
1937	Heede (Germany)	4 children		No decision
1937	Voltago (Italy)	2 people		Negative decision
1937	Bettin (Italy)	1 man		No decision
1937	Oberbruck (France)	Teen-age girl		No decision
1937	*Heede-im-Emsland* (Germany)	4 girls	**Yes**	No decision
1937	Saint-Bonnet (France)	Teen-age girl		No decision
1937	*Tre Fontane* (Italy)	Young girl		No decision

1938	Saint-Pierre-la-Cour (France)	N.A.		No decision
1938	Madrid (Spain)	Young girl		No decision
1938	Wangen/Wigratzbad (Germany)	1 woman	**Yes**	No decision
1938	Kerizinen (France)	1 woman		Negative decision
1938	Bochum (Germany)	1 woman		No decision
1938	Oberpleis (Germany)	1 woman		No decision
1939	Kerrytown (Ireland)	Crowd		No decision
1939	Dublin (Ireland)	N.A.		No decision
1939	Saint-Placide (Canada)	1 girl		No decision
1940	Marienfried (Germany)	1 girl	**Yes**	No decision
1940	Ortoncourt (France)	1 girl		No decision
1940	Bodonnou (France)	1 girl		No decision
1941	Alto de Umbe (Spain)	1 woman		No decision
1942	Cornamona (Irelande)	1 girl		No decision
1943	Girkalnis (Lithuania)	Crowd		Negative decision
1943	Athis-Mons (France)	Crowd		Negative decision
1943	Vernet-la-Varenne	2 children		No decision

	(France)			
1944	*Ghiaie-di-Bonate* (Italy)	1 girl		<u>Negative decision</u>
1944	Detroit (U.S.A.)	1 woman		No decision
1945	Amsterdam (Holland)	1 woman	**Yes**	<u>Yes</u>
1945	Codosera (Spain)	1 girl & 1 seers	**Yes**	No decision
1945	Vilar Chao (Portugal)	1 woman		No decision
1946	*Ile Pasman* (Yugoslavia)	Numerous seers		No decision
1946	Espis (France)	2 girls		Negative decision
1947	*Tre Fontane* (Italy)	1 man & 3 children	**Yes**	No decision
1947	Montichiari (Italy)	1 woman		Negative decision
1947	Casanova Staffora (Italy)	1 girl		Negative decision
1947	Vorstenbosch (Holland)	3 children		No decision
1947	Emmerichberg (Hungary)	1 woman		No decision
1947	Tannhausen (Germany)	1 woman		No decision
1947	Kayl (Luxembourg)	1 girl		No decision
1947	L'Ile-Bouchard (France)	4 girls	**Yes**	No decision
1947	Plescop (France)	3 girls		No decision
1947	Bolzanet (Italy)	N.A.		No decision

1947	Gallinaro (Italy)	1 person		No decision
1947	Gramolazzo (Italy)	1 person		No decision
1947	Varzi (Italy)	1 girl		No decision
1947	Forsweiler (Germany)	1 woman & 4 children		Negative decision
1947	Arcachon (France)	a child		Negative decision
1947	Grottamare (Italy)	a child		No decision
1947	Ile-Napolean (France)	3 children		No decision
1947	Montepoli (Italy)	1 woman		No decision
1947	Munich (Germany)	1 woman		No decision
1947	Tyromestice (Slovakia)	3 shepherds		No decision
1947	Trois-Rivieres (Canada)	1 man		No decision
1947	Urucaina (Brazil)	1 religious		Negative decision
1948	Marta (Italy)	Children		Negative decision
1948	Gimigliano (Italy)	Teen-age girl		Negative decision
1948	Marina di Pisa (Italy)	Crowd		No decision
1948	Ponsacco (Italy)	N.A.		No decision
1948	Remola (Italy)	A child		No decision
1948	Rome (Italy)	Teen-age boy		No decision

1948	Castelmadama (Italy)	N.A.		No decision
1948	Zischowicz (Czechoslovaki a)	3 girls		No decision
1948	Lipa (Philippines)	1 religious		Negative decision
1948	Montlucon (France)	1 religious		Negative decision
1948	Aspang (Austria)	1 man		No decision
1948	Liart (France)	Crowd		No decision
1948	Saint-Jean-aux-Bois (France)	1 woman		No decision
1948	La Forclaz (France)	1 man		No decision
1948	Cluj (Romania)	Crowd		Negative decision
1948	Frascati (Italy)	N.A.		No decision
1948	Liceta (Italy)	N.A.		No decision
1948	Lucca (Italy)	Crowd		No decision
1948	Nocera Superiore (Italy)	A child		No decision
1949	Dueren (Germany)	1 woman		No decision
1949	Lublin (Poland)	Crowd		Negative decision
1949	Zo-Se (China)	1 religious		Negative decision
1949	Fehrbach (Germany)	Teen-age girl		Negative decision

1949	Bergalla (Italy)	N.A.		No decision
1949	Loano (Italy)	N.A.		No decision
1949	Hasznos (Hungary)	Crowd		Negative decision
1949	Montreal (Canada)	1 religious		No decision
1949	Dublin (Ireland)	N.A.		No decision
1949	Balestrino (Italy)	1 woman		Negative decision
1949	Palmira (Columbia)	A young boy		No decision
1949	Bogota (Columbia)	1 religious		No decision
1949	Gimigliano (Italy)	A young girl		Negative decision
1949	Heroldsbach (Germany)	Four children		Negative decision
1949	Weert (Holland)	1 person		No decision
1949	Sonnenhalb (Switzerland)	1 woman		No decision
1949	Wurzburg (Germany)	1 religious		No decision
1949	Necedah (U.S.A.)	1 woman		Negative decision
1950	Acquaviva Platani (Italy)	Teen-age girl		Negative decision
1950	Saint-Eugène de Gamby (Canada)	3 children		No decision
1950	Ribera (Italy)	2 children		No decision
1950	Denver (U.S.A.)	Teen-age girl		No decision

1950	Remagen (Germany)	20 children		No decision
1950	Perregaux (Algeria)	1 woman		No decision
1950	Guarciano (Italy)	A child		No decision
1950	Casalicchio (Italy)	Young girl		No decision
1950	Binghamton (U.S.A.)	1 woman		No decision
1950	Belmuttet (Ireland)	Teen-age girl		No decision
1950	Bienvenuda-Usagre (Spain)	1 man		No decision
1950	Padoue (Italy)	1 woman		No decision
1951	Amarossi (Italy)	Teen-age girl		No decision
1951	Arluno (Italy)	1 woman		No decision
1951	Oriolo Calabro (Italy)	1 man		No decision
1951	Casali contrada (Italy)	1 man		Negative decision
1951	Dugny (France)	3 people		No decision
1951	Tangua (Brazil)	Young girl		No decision
1951	Tinos (Greece)	N.A.		No decision
1951	Baggio (Italy)	Young girl		No decision
1952	Bergame (Italy)	1 woman		No decision
1952	Orria (Italy)	Crowd		No decision
1952	Rome (Italy)	1 woman		No decision
1952	Rodalben (Germany)	1 woman		No decision

1952	Niederbach (Germany)	1 man		No decision
1952	Gerpinnes (Belgium)	Young girl		No decision
1952	Nyakijoga-Ambucoba, Tanzania (Africa)	Many persons		No decision
1953	Cossirano (Italy)	Young girl		Negative decision
1953	Bivigliano (Italy)	1 man		No decision
1953	Hubersent (France)	3 children/1 adult		Negative decision
1953	Santo Saba (Italy)	Young boy		Negative decision
1953	Rome (Italy)	Teen-age girl		No decision
1953	Philadelphia (U.S.A)	1 woman		No decision
1953	Frignano Maggiore (Italy)	Teen-age girl		No decision
1953	Calabro di Mileto (Italy)	1 woman		No decision
1953	*Sabana Grande* (Porta Rico)	3 children		No decision
1953	Syracuse (Italy)	1 man & 1woman		**Yes**
1953	Dubovytsya (Ukraine)	1 woman		No decision
1954	Seredne (Ukraine)	Several people		No decision

1954	Catane (Italy)	A boy		No decision
1954	Vittoria (Italy)	2 sisters		No decision
1954	Mezzolombardo (Italy)	1 man		No decision
1954	Palerme (Italy)	Several children		No decision
1954	Sasso Marconi (Italy)	1 woman		No decision
1954	Marche-en-Famenne (Belgium)	N.A.		No decision
1954	Eisenberg (Austria)	Young girl		Negative decision
1954	Colombera di Avenza (Italy)	1 man		No decision
1954	Pingsdorf (Germany)	2 women		No decision
1954	Saint-Tropez (France)	N.A.		No decision
1954	Rome (Italy)	1 woman		No decision
1954	Newcastle (Great Britain)	N.A.		No decision
1954	Bande (Luxembourg)	Several children		No decision
1954	Cosenza (Italy)	1 religious		No decision
1954	Ibdes (Spain)	Several children		No decision
1954	Pombia (Italy)	1 woman		No decision
1955	Reggio Emilia (Italy)	1 woman		Negative decision
1955	Itauna (Brazil)	1 man		No decision
1955	San Vincenzo	1 woman		No decision

	(Italy)			
1955	Eisenberg-a-Raab (Austria)	1 woman		Negative decision
1955	Rome (Italy)	1 woman		No decision
1955	Ngom, (South Africa)	1 religious	**Yes**	No decision
1956	Assoro (Italy)	4 children		No decision
1956	Fostoria, Ohio (USA)	Sister Mildred Neuzil	Yes	No decision
1956	Urbania (Italy)	Several children		Negative decision
1957	Sausalito (U.S.A.)	1 man		No decision
1957	Cracovie (Poland)	1 woman		No decision
1957	Gasp, (Canada)	N.A.		No decision
1958	Jorcas (Spain)	N.A.		No decision
1958	Villa Barone (Italy)	1 woman		No decision
1958	Turczovka (Slovakia)	1 man		No decision
1958	Vallemaio (Italy)	1 family		No decision
1958	Mantoue (Italy)	A child		No decision
1958	Milan (Italy)	N.A.		No decision
1958	Terni (Italy)	2 children		No decision
1959	Scheggia (Italy)	4 children		No decision
1959	Vibo Valentia (Italy)	Young boy		No decision
1959	Varsovie	Several		No decision

	(Poland)	people	
1959	Stornarella (Italy)	1 man	No decision
1959	Ascona (Switzerland)	N.A.	No decision
1960	Acqua Voltri (Italy)	A boy	No decision
1960	Paravati (Italy)	N.A.	No decision
1960	Thierenbach (France)	1 man	No decision
1960	Jungholtz (France)	1 man, Fernand Llakay	No decision
1960	Neuwier, Allemagne, Bade-Wurtembur	1 person	No decision
1961	Garabandal (Spain)	4 girls	Negative decision
1961	Brigueil-le-Chantre (France)	Teen-age girl	No decision
1961	Craveggia (Italy)	1 woman	Negative decision
1961	San Damiano (Italy)	1 woman	Negative decision
1961	Casalicontrada (Italy)	1 girl, Eleonora Fasoli	No decision
1962	Skiemonys (Lithuania)	Teen-age girl	No decision
1962	Ladeira (Portugal)	1 woman	Negative decision

1962	Chiari(Italy)	1 woman		No decision
1962	Jaddico (Italy)	Many persons		No decision
1962	Monte Fasce (Italy)	Two people		No decision
1963	Verceil (Italy)	2 men		No decision
1964	San Vittorino Roman (Italy)	N.A.	**Yes**	No decision
1964	Turczovka (Slovakia)	1 man		No decision
1965	Fribourg (Switzerland)	A girl		No decision
1965	Conchar (Spain)	1 woman		No decision
1966	Porto-San-Stefano (Italy)	1 man		No decision
1966	Ain-el-Del (Lebanon)	Teen-age boy		No decision
1966	Cabra (Philippines)	Teen-age girl		No decision
1966	Liège (Belgium)	N.A.		No decision
1966	Rome (Italy)	Teen-age girl		No decision
1966	Ventebbio (Italy)	1 priest		Negative decision
1967	Nativitade (Brazil)	1 man		No decision
1967	Cefala Diana (Italy)	4 children	**Yes**	No decision
1967	Raccula (Italy)	N.A.		No decision
1967	Fribourg (Switzerland)	1 woman		No decision

175

1967	Bohan (Belgium)	2 men		Negative decision
1967	Mont-Laurier (Canada)	1 woman		No decision
1967	Quebec (Canada)	1 girl		No decision
1967	Oulx (Italy)	1 woman		No decision
1968	*St-Bruno-de-Chambly* (Canada)	Several children		No decision
1968	Anse-aux-Gascons (Canada)	Several children		No decision
1968	Fort Kent (U.S.A.)	Young boy		No decision
1968	Maille (France)	4 children		No decision
1968	*Palmar de Troya* (Spain)	4 young girls		Negative decision
1968	Zeitoun (Egypt)	Crowd		**Yes**
1968	Mexico	Many people		No Decision
1969	Florence (Italy)	1 person		No decision
1969	Barcelona (Spain)	N.A.		No decision
1969	Mexico (Mexico)	1 religious		No decision
1969	Dayton, Ohio (U.S.A.)	3 persons		No decision
1969	U.S.A.	1 person		No decision
1970	Milan (Italy)	Several people		No decision
1970	Sherbroke	N.A.		No decision

	(Canada)			
1970	Limal (Belgium)	1 man		No decision
1970	Maropati (Italy)	1 woman		No decision
1970	Lecce (Italy)	Teen-age boy		Negative decision
1970	Bayside (U.S.A.)	1 woman		Negative decision
1970	Vladimir (Russia)	1 man		No decision
1971	Belpasso (Italy)	Teen-age boy		No decision
1971	Pendiamo (Columbia)	Young girl		No decision
1971	Crèteil (France)	N.A.		No decision
1971	Luke Saint John (Canada)	N.A.		No decision
1971	San Vicens del Horts (Spain)	1 man		No decision
1971	Monte Umbe (Spain)	1 person		No decision
1971	Ngome (Africa)	1 person		No decision
1972	El Mimbral (Spain)	Several people		No decision
1972	Porziano (Italy)	Several people		No decision
1972	Ravenna (Italy)	Several children		No decision
1972	Drummondville (Canada)	N.A.		No decision
1972	Madrid (Spain)	Two people		No decision
1973	Akita (Japan)	1 religious		Yes
1973	Nitape (Peru)	1 religious &		No decision

		several children		
1973	Mortzel (Belgium)	N.A.		Negative decision
1974	Dozul, (France)	1 woman		Negative decision
1974	Derval (France)	1 man		Negative decision
1974	Gallinaro (Italy)	1 person		No decision
1974	Cinquefrondi (Italy)	1 woman		No decision
1975	Dugny (France)	Teen-age girl		No decision
1975	Binh Trieu (Vietnam)	1 man		No decision
1976	Cerdanyola (Spain)	N.A.		Negative decision
1976	Betania (Venezuela)	1 woman		**Yes**
1976	Olmos (Peru)	Young girl		Negative decision
1976	Puylaurens (France)	1 man		Negative decision
1976	Rome (Italy)	1 girl		No decision
1976	Rome (Italy)	1 person		No decision
1977	Rostov (U.S.S.R.)	N.A.		No decision
1977	Kharkov (U.S.S.R.)	N.A.		No decision
1977	Leningrad (U.S.S.R.)	N.A.		No decision
1977	Le Fréchou (France)	1 man		Negative decision

1977	Lamezia Terne (Italy)	Young man		No decision
1980	Cuapa (Nicaragua)	1 man	**Yes**	**Yes**
1980	El Escorial (Spain)	1 woman		Negative decision
1980	Ede Oballa (Nigeria)	1 man		Negative decision
1980	Wu Fung Chi (Taiwan)	9 men		No decision
1980	Alaska (U.S.A.)	1 man		No decision
1981	Medjugorje (Bosnia-Herzegovinia)	Several people		No final decision
1981	La Talaudière (France)	Young girl		Negative decision
1981	Kibèho (Rwanda)	Teen-agers	**Yes**	**Yes**
1981	Seoul (Korea)	1 woman		No decision
1981	Rome (Italy)	1 woman		No decision
1982	Izbicno (Bosnia-Herzegovinia)	2 children		No decision
1982	Arguello (Argentina)	1 man, then several others		No decision
1982	Damascus (Syria)	1 woman		No decision
1982	Nowra (Australia)	1 man		Negative decision
1982	Milan (Italy)	Father Stephano Gobbi		No decision

179

1982	Canton (U.S.A.)	1 woman		Negative decision
1983	Penablanca (Chili)	Teen-age boy		Negative decision
1983	San Nicolas (Argentina)	1 woman	**Yes**	**Yes**
1983	Olawa (Poland)	1 man		Negative decision
1983	Surbiton (Great Britain)	1 woman		No decision
1983	Moncalieri (Italy)	1 man		No decision
1983	Louisiana (U.S.A.)	1 woman		No decision
1983	Beit Sahour (Israel)	Many persons		No decision
1984	Kernéguez (France)	1 woman		No decision
1984	Montpinchon (France)	Several people		No decision
1984	Jall-el-Dib (Lebanon)	Young girl		No decision
1984	Gargallo di Carpi (Italy)	1 man		Negative decision
1984	Crotone (Italy)	Several people		No decision
1984	Mushasha (Burundi)	1 man		No decision
1984	Kinshasa (Zaire)	1 man		No decision
1984	Bakersfield (U.S.A.)	Crowd		No decision
1985	Lvov (Ukraine)	N.A.		No decision

1985	Melleray (Ireland)	3 children		No decision
1985	Carns (Ireland)	4 girls		No decision
1985	Schio (Italy)	1 man		Negative decision
1985	Oliveta Citra (Italy)	8 children		No decision
1985	Sofferetti (Italy)	Several people		No decision
1985	Bisceglie (Italy)	Young girl		No decision
1985	Belluno (Italy)	2 teen-agers		No decision
1985	Floridia (Italy)	8 children		No decision
1985	Casavatore (Italy)	Several children		No decision
1985	Cleveland (U.S.A.)	1 woman		No decision
1986	Mazzano (Italy)	1 woman		No decision
1986	Cardito (Italy)	Teen-age girl		No decision
1986	Sezze (Italy)	Several people		No decision
1986	Belpasso (Italy)	Teen-age boy		No decision
1986	Campobasso (Italy)	N.A.		No decision
1986	Giubasco (Italy)	1 man		No decision
1986	Verviers (Belgium)	N.A.		No decision
1986	Nsimalen (Cameroon)	6 children		Negative decision
1986	Bilychi	2 men		No decision

	(Ukraine)			
1986	Santa Fe (U.S.A.)	1 woman		No decision
1986	Manila (Philippines)	soldiers		No decision
1986	Balestrino (Italy)	1 girl, Caterina Richero		No decision
1987	Borgosesia (Italy)	1 man		No decision
1987	Hrushiv (Ukraine)	Teen-age girl		No decision
1987	Zarvanystya (Ukraine)	Several people		No decision
1987	Pochayiv (Ukraine)	Several people		No decision
1987	Port-a-Prince (Haiti)	1 religious		No decision
1987	Esmeraldas (Ecuador)	Teen-age boy		No decision
1987	Inchigeela (Ireland)	2 young girls		No decision
1987	Bessbrock (Ireland)	1 woman & 1 boy		No decision
1987	Mayfield (Ireland)	Two girls		No decision
1987	Granstown (Ireland)	Two girls		No decision
1987	Cortnadreha (Ireland)	Young girl		No decision
1987	Mulevala (Mozambique)	Crowd		No decision
1987	Belpasso (Italy)	Teen-age		No decision

		boy		
1987	Crosia (Italy)	2 teen-agers		No decision
1987	Terra Blanca (Mexico)	3 children		No decision
1987	Pennsylvania U.S.A.)	1 man		No decision
1988	Achill (Ireland)	Christina Gallagher	Negative decision	Negative decision
1988	Hustusco (Mexico)	3 people		No decision
1988	Lubbock (U.S.A.)	Several people		Negative decision
1988	Scottsdale (U.S.A.)	Several people		Negative decision
1988	Phoenix (U.S.A.)	1 woman		Negative decision
1988	Grosby (U.S.A.)	N.A.		No decision
1988	Tikfaw (U.S.A.)	1 man		No decision
1988	El Cajas (Ecuador)	1 girl		No decision
1989	Burlington (Canada)	1 man		No decision
1989	Agoo (Philippines)	Teen-age boy		No decision
1989	Marlboro (U.S.A.)	1 man		No decision
1989	Florence (Italy)	1 person		Negative decision
1990	Denver (U.S.A.)	Theresa Lopez		Negative decision
1990	Conyers	Nancy		No decision

	(U.S.A.)	Fowler		
1990	Kurescek (Slovene)	Father Stephan		No decision
1990	Hillside (U.S.A.)	Joseph Reinholtz		No decision
1990	Litmanova (Slovakia)	Vetka Korcakova Katka Ceselkova		No decision
1990	Beaumont-du-Ventoux (France)	1 woman		No decision
1991	Holving (France)	N.A.		No decision
1991	Mozul (Iraq)	Dina Basher		No decision
1991	Woombe (Australia)	Susanna D'Amore		No decision
1991	Arkansas/Texas (U.S.A.)	1 woman		No decision
1991	San Juan (Puerto Rico)	Luz Diaz		No decision
1991	Lake Ridge (U.S.A.)	Father James Bruse		No decision
1991	San Bruno (U.S.A.)	Carlos Lopez Jorge Zavala		No decision
1991	Paris (France)	Two people		No decision
1992	Moscow (Russia)	N.A.		No decision
1992	Falmouth (U.S.A.)	Sandy		No decision

1992	Toledo (U.S.A.)	Sally Steadman		No decision
1992	Scottsdale (U.S.A.)	Carole Ameche Peterson		No decision
1992	Enfield (U.S.A.)	Neil Harrington Jr.		No decision
1992	Aokpe (Nigeria)	Christina Agbo		<u>No final decision</u>
1993	Thu Duc (Vietnam)	1 girl		No decision
1993	Arc-Watripont (Belgium)	1 boy		No decision
1993	Belleville (U.S.A.)	Roy Doiron		No decision
1993	Cincinnati (U.S.A.)	Rita Ring woman		N.A.
1993	New S. Wales (Australia)	Matthew Kelly		No decision
1993	Rochester (U.S.A.)	1 man		No decision
1994	Dechtice (Slovakia)	Martin Gavenda Maria Gavendova Lucia Vadikova Martina Kalasova Adrianna Kudelova Simona Kumpanova Jozef Danko		No decision

1994	Emmitsburg (U.S.A.)	Gianna Talone-Sullivan		Negative decision
1995	Sterling (U.S.A.)	Patricia Mundorf		No decision
1995	Ham Lake (U.S.A.)	Little Mary		No decision
1995	Enugu State (Nigeria)	1 man		No decision
1996	Bahia (Brazil)	Fabiana Oliveira		No decision
1996	Brooklyn (U.S.A.)	1 man		No decision
1996	Elyria (U.S.A.)	Maureen Sweeney Kyle		Negative decision
1996	Bachaquero Zulia (Venezuela)	1 person		No decision
1997	Minnesota (U.S.A.)	Rev. Andrew Wingate		No decision
1997	Platina (Brazil)	Francisco Ovidio da Salva		No decision
1997	El Dorado (U.S.A.)	Augustine Halverson		No decision
1997	Satua (Samoa)	Suor Ruth Augustus		No decision
1997	Mexico City (Mexico)	1 man		No decision
1998	Greenfield (U.S.A.)	John Snide		No decision
1998	St. John's	Don Gerard		No decision

	(Antigua)	Critch		
1998	Montreal (Canada)	Delmis		No decision
1998	Saskatoon (Canada)	Carmen Humphrey		No decision
1999	Marpingen (Germany)	Christine Ney Marion Guttma Judith Hiber		No decision
1999	Montsurs (France)	Agnes Marie		No decision
1999	Pennsylvania (U.S.A.)	Louise Starr Tomkiel		No decision
1999	Staten Island (U.S.A.)	Carmelo Cortez		No decision
1999	Arma (Italy)	1 young girl		No decision
2000	El Algarrobal (Argentina)	Manuel Yanzon		Negative decision
2000	Prince Edward Island (Canada)	Father Melvin Doucette		No decision
2001	Hilversum (Netherlands)	Agatha Moiki		No decision
2001	Skaneateles (U.S.A.)	Mary Sheila Reilly		No decision
2007	Johannesburg (South Africa)	Francesca Zackey		No decision
2007	Velipojes (Albania)	Valmira Malaj		No decision

Epilogue

Marian apparitions are a constant event, normally occurring in several places, worldwide, at the same time. The Medjugorie experience is still active after twenty-nine years. The Pope has recently announced that there will be a commission established to validate Medjugorie. Some clerics, though, say there will never be a ruling on validity till the apparitions cease at Medjugorie.

Cardinal Christoph Schönborn of Vienna, a very influential cardinal, has given support to the authenticity of the Medjugorie apparitions. He signaled this support by visiting Medjugorie in a 2010 visit. Though the cardinal did not want to interject himself into a declaration of authenticity, he diplomatically still showed his positive view of Medjugorie.

Another ongoing discussion is whether the famous third secret of Fatima has been fully revealed. The Vatican announcement of the third secret, in 2001, dealt with the assassination attempt on Pope John Paul II. Many referred to as "Fatimists", insist that Mary's warnings were apocalyptic. Some even think the church's child abuse crisis was foretold at Fatima. A recent conference was held in May 2010 in Rome, dealing with Fatima issues. Christopher Ferrara is a Catholic, and U.S. attorney. He was quoted at the conference as saying, "The evidence points to only one conclusion: that something has to be missing...(only a minority) cling steadfastly to the notion that an ambiguous vision of a bishop dressed in white outside a half-ruined city is all there is to the third secret". (Catholic News Service)

The notion, held by the Fatimists, is that the Vatican has withheld details of apocalyptic warnings, not wanting to cause panic. An alternate insight is that the church has withheld abuse warnings, to avoid embarrassment. Popes have held the details of the "third secret" in their private files for years. It does seem peculiar to maintain secrecy for such a supposedly murky prophecy.

Brazil has produced a seer in Pedro Regis. He claims to have been receiving apparitions of Mary since 1987. He has made some rather startling prophecies regarding an increase in earthquakes. Certainly, the last two years have seen phenomenal earthquakes, especially the events in Haiti. Time will tell if this is a legitimate apparition, though it looks genuine on the surface.

Another round of apparitions have occurred in Cairo. This time the location was in Warraq El-Hadar, an island in the Nile, part of Cairo. On December 22, 2009, apparitions very similar to Zeitoun were seen over Virgin Mary and Archangel Michael Coptic Church. They are easily viewed on YouTube. Extensive local media coverage has been devoted to covering this story.

The Bishop of Giza issued the following statement: "The Bishopric of Giza announces that the Holy Virgin has appeared in a transfiguration at the church named after her in Warraq El-Hadar, Giza, in the early hours of Friday, "December 2009 at 1:00 am. The Holy Virgin appeared in her full height in luminous robes, above the middle dome of the church, in pure white dress and a royal blue belt. She had a crown on her head, above which appeared the cross on top of the dome. The crosses on top of the church's domes and towers glowed brightly with light. The Holy Virgin moved between the domes and on to the top of the church gate between its two twin towers. The local residents all saw her. The apparition lasted from 1:00 am till 4:00 am Friday, and was registered by cameras and cell phones. Some 3000 people from the neighborhood, surrounding areas, and passers-by gathered in the street in front of the church to see the apparition".

A further quote from Bishop Theodosios of Giza states: "I stayed up all night on Sunday. I saw doves appear suddenly in the sky. They flew in circles in front of the church before they vanished into thin air. They were floating rather than hovering with their wings". (zeitioun.org).

The dramatic natures of the recent Cairo apparitions are almost identical to the 1968-1970 Zeitoun ones. Given the obvious nature of the display, Coptic officials have authenticated their validity.

The Virgin Mary's mission as our Mother is ongoing. God still loves us, and sends His representatives to a reluctant mankind.

6248739R0

Made in the USA
Lexington, KY
02 August 2010